I0679558

Roller Rubout

(A Josephine Stuart Mystery)

by

Joyce Oroz

This book is fiction. All characters, events, and organizations portrayed in this novel are the product of the author's imagination or are used fictitiously. Any resemblance to actual persons—living or dead—is entirely coincidental.

Copyright 2014 by Joyce Oroz

All rights reserved. No parts of this book may be reproduced or transmitted in any form or by any means, electronic or mechanical, including photocopying, recording or by any information storage and retrieval system, without written permission from the author, except for the inclusion of brief quotations in a review.

For information, email **Cozy Cat Press**, cozycatpress@aol.com or visit our website at: www.cozycatpress.com

COZY CAT
P R E S S

ISBN: 978-1-939816-53-5

Printed in the United States of America

Cover design by Keri Knutson
http://www.alchemybookcovers.com/

1 2 3 4 5 6 7 8 9 10

Acknowledgements

I want to thank my crew of dedicated friends and family who helped me with this book. What would I do without Tomiko Edmiston, the lady who cleans up my manuscript and prepares it for print? Thank you, Tomi, with all my heart. And thank you Tech-team, Avery, Michael and Jeff for keeping my computer alive and well. Thank you, Manuel Oroz, for the pictures and explanation of the safe. Thank you to the Derby Girls for their inspiration. And Art, thank you for all your suggestions and for putting up with my writing time, holed up in the dungeon. I'm glad one of us has good logic and common sense (I didn't say which one). Last but not least, thank you Cozy Cat Press and Patricia Rockwell for publishing my book.

CHAPTER ONE

Disaster struck Wednesday, my second day on the job at Ralph's Roller Rink located on the east side of Santa Cruz, California. A hit-and-run driver, most likely over eighty, hit the gas instead of the brake according to police. *The Sentinel* reported that a car slammed through exterior walls and an inner office. Employee Mario Portello died at his desk. The car finally came to a stop against a sixty-year-old steel stall in the ladies' restroom. Still in a geriatric daze, the driver found reverse and has not been seen since.

I was the only witness at the rink that sunny morning in May. It happened so fast I barely saw the black sedan covered in roller rink residue topped off with a pair of size ten loafers. A well-trained chimpanzee could have been driving for all I knew. The windshield had been a magnet for shredded building materials and powdered wallboard.

My first thought was, "Is this a movie stunt?" My second thought ... "Run!"

The crashing noises were deafening behind me as I sprinted twenty yards to the back door, still gripping a drippy stir stick in my white-knuckled fist. I looked over my shoulder in time to see the vehicle backing through a massive hole in the wall, back to daylight, sidewalks and unsuspecting pedestrians. I heard the tires squeal and smelled rubber.

The only rooms still standing in the cavernous building were two restrooms. The office had been flattened into a pile of debris.

My stubborn interrogator, Sergeant Fishburn, had a preconceived idea about how Mr. Portello lost his life. No matter how I described what I had seen, the officer was sure the driver was an out-of-control oldster, a senile senior probably heading for Bonnie's Bingo Parlor two doors away. Since I didn't see through the windshield, I couldn't describe the driver; consequently, I was unable to convince Fishburn that there had been foul play.

Painting the musical notes and words to the "Hokey Pokey" across a sixty-foot light-blue wall was not my worst-ever mural job, but close to it. Tuesday, my first day on the job, was spent measuring, taping and calculating on paper. Ralph Rattini, owner of the roller rink, had given me very specific hours. Painting had to end before three o'clock when school was out and the kids would come charging in, and the entire job needed to be finished before the big roller derby event on Memorial Day. That gave us three weeks.

Just before I slipped out the back door at three o'clock, I glanced across the enormous room. Mario Portello, a slight gentleman, short and balding, left his little office, walked to the main entrance and unlocked the doors to let in hoards of young skaters. Two teenage boys were the first to enter. Mario greeted them and pointed to their assigned duties behind the counter. It was my first look at Mr. Portello … and my last.

Wednesday's work, mixing colors of paint and drawing a pepper tree near the back door, was cut short when the infamous black sedan struck. After that, my hands were not steady enough to draw or paint, and thinking was out of the question.

Sergeant Fishburn questioned me relentlessly and finally said, "Go home, Ms. Stuart. You'll feel better tomorrow." I detected a bit of kindness in his voice. Maybe he felt sorry for me because I shivered every time I recalled details of the shocking ordeal.

My employees, Alicia and Kyle, were unable to join me until Thursday. Alicia had jury duty and Kyle had the flu. Alicia was my best friend, a wonderful painter and looked like a model. Kyle was a student at the University in Santa Cruz, a talented painter and a shy young gentleman. Alicia had a husband, Ernie, and a ten-year-old son, Trigger. Kyle had spiky red hair, tattoos and piercings up and down his lanky body.

Thursday morning, Alicia arrived at the rink looking like a Latina movie star, except for the paint-streaked clothes and rubber flip-flops.

"Hi, Jo. You told me the place was trashed, but I had to see it to believe how bad it is. Are the owners back from the islands yet?" Alicia looked across an ocean of shiny wood flooring to the temporarily boarded up hole next to the main entrance and shook her head slowly. She turned back, saw me preparing for work and immediately helped me lay tarps along the south wall. We needed to protect the floor—after all, people paid good money to roller skate on the smooth surface.

"The owners aren't back yet but the carpenters are coming today. Things will get back to normal pretty soon … except for poor Mr. Portello." I glanced at the rubble that used to be his office. "I think he was the bookkeeper or something. He sold the place to Ralph five years ago; but he stayed on as an employee, according to *The Sentinel*."

"Maybe our mural will bring back some happiness to this old place," Alicia said. "I used to skate here when I was a kid."

"Yeah, me too, but that was before you were born."

"Jo, being fifty isn't so bad. It's the new thirty," she laughed. "Did they do the Hokey Pokey when you were a kid?"

"Yes, and I thought it was old fashioned even then."

I smiled as skating memories flooded my mind. Just the smell of the old building sent flashes of friends, embarrassing moments and a freezer full of popsicles, which everyone lined up for after fifty thousand circles around the rink. But Hokey Pokey memories were the clearest. The announcer had us form a circle in the middle of the floor and the music told us what to do as we sang along.

"You put your right foot in, you put your right foot out, do the Hokey Pokey and turn yourself about. That's what it's all about," Alicia sang, and like everything else, she did it beautifully.

Kyle arrived in the middle of our giggles, looking like a college kid who needed to earn some rent money. The design on his retro black t-shirt featured one yellow word, "Nukes," ringed and slashed in red. He had parked his yellow Honda motorcycle in the back lot with our vehicles and entered the building through the back door.

"Josephine, like, what happened? This place is a mess." He stared at the pile of rubble, the boarded up hole in the wall and yellow tape everywhere along the west side of the skating area.

"Did I forget to tell you? A UFO landed here," I said.

"Actually there was a hit-and-run driver yesterday," Alicia added.

Kyle's jaw dropped. "Wow!"

"The owner of the rink called me from Maui last night. He and his wife are waiting for a plane to Oahu so they can fly home. He didn't sound too happy about coming back so soon, and he told me to start work as planned. He wants this place in good shape before Memorial Day. Apparently, they have a big skating party on the weekend. We have fourteen workdays to finish our mural."

"Don't worry, Josephine. We can do it," Kyle said, as he and Alicia headed for the back parking lot. Alicia stopped halfway to the door and turned around.

"Jo, wasn't your boss upset about Mr. Portello's death?"

"Ralph didn't mention it. Maybe he's in shock." I shrugged.

After two trips, my painterly friends and I had emptied the truck and carried all the paint supplies inside. Unfortunately, I was unable to get permission to store anything at the rink overnight. Apparently, they didn't have an extra closet or shelf we could use. We would have to cart everything back and forth, thirty-five miles from my house in Aromas to the Santa Cruz location on Seabright Avenue. Everyday!

My next-door neighbor and close friend, David Galaz, was the reason I got the mural job. He knew Ralph from high school, and they ran into each other now and then. A couple months ago, they had a beer together; and Ralph told David his plans to improve the rink. Ralph talked wallpaper. David talked murals. In the end, my company, Wildbrush Murals, had a nice contract.

According to David, Ralph's favorite memories of the rink happened over thirty years ago when he met his wife while doing the "Hokey Pokey." As a teenager, Ralph had worked at the counter renting out skates and occasionally helping Mario herd the skaters to the middle of the floor for the Hokey Pokey routine.

Sixteen-year-old Ashley put her right foot in, shook it all about and fell down. Eighteen-year-old Ralph helped her off the floor and over to the freezer full of popsicles and ice packs. She had both and felt better. They had been a couple ever since.

Naturally, my design for the long southern wall was centered around that old-time song. The scale drawing showed five horizontal lines full of Hokey Pokey notes and words running the length of the sixty-foot wall, above the handrail. Above and behind the music, I planned to have puffy clouds here and there and seagulls in flight—seagulls being synonymous with Santa Cruz and the beach.

When we finished arranging the paint, ladders and equipment on top of the tarps, I called a meeting. Alicia became the designated cloud painter because her clouds were always heavenly. Kyle and I would help, following her lead and especially her style.

Once the clouds were finished, I would draw the staff and five parallel lines using chalk and a level. Kyle would paint them since his hands were young and steady, while Alicia and I added seagulls to the upper areas. When the lines were finished, I would draw a thirty-inch clef and dozens of giant-size notes copied from an old song sheet. The Hokey Pokey words would be painted below the notes in large black print.

Ralph also wanted me to paint the sides of the ancient counter where people rented skates. I suggested faux redwood planks with a simulated marble finish on the counter top. The fake wood-and-marble job was not time-sensitive. I would start it when I had time.

Police investigators shuffled around in the debris that used to be Mr. Portello's office while we worked along the south wall under a long stretch of very high windows. Beating through the glass was an unusually hot sun for the month of May. Funny thing about the California Coast—we enjoyed moderate temperatures except for the random week in May and the ones in December and February where the temperature and humidity pushed into the high eighties. We were two days into the blazing random week.

I crossed the expansive wood floor and found the old water fountain, rusted but otherwise unharmed. The water felt good when I splashed it on my face. I looked up at the officer coming my way. It was Sergeant Fishburn. I noticed his hair was starting to grey and there was an extra little layer around his middle, but as mid-lifers go, he looked pretty good. He had good posture, broad shoulders and a nice smile, but nothing compared to David, of course.

"Ms. Stuart, I don't suppose you have seen the driver of the black sedan...."

"I know you want me to let you know if I see the driver; but, like I told you, I never saw the driver in the first place, too much stuff on the windshield. I really don't think it was an accident because...." As Fishburn turned away to answer his phone, my words dissolved into a whisper.

"Sorry, that call was important. Now, where were we?" He pocketed the phone.

"Sergeant, have you checked out Bonnie's Bingo Parlor yet?" I said this with a straight face and did not roll my eyes.

"I don't believe that will be necessary. Our work here is just about finished. I'm going to let a crew of workmen come in this afternoon to clean up the place before the carpenters arrive tomorrow." He smiled his charming smile and joined another detective who was examining the still-standing ladies' restroom stall.

I wiped sweat from my brow, splashed more water over my face and arms, and tried to remember what Fishburn had just told me; but all I knew for sure was that his eyes were the color of a bay in the Bahamas.

As I rejoined my cohorts, I heard a few snorts and giggles.

"Checking out the officer, Jo?" Alicia laughed, as she backed down the ladder.

"Well, he's not hard on the eyes ... actually I went over there for a drink. I was so hot that I ended up splashing water all over myself. I was afraid Fishburn would arrest me for dribbling water on the floor."

"He wouldn't do that, would he?" Kyle said, while Alicia rolled her eyes to the rafters. "Alicia said you saw the accident happen."

"Part of that is true. I saw it happen but it was no accident."

"You really think someone did this on purpose?" Alicia asked.

"All I know is it would take great skill to back through a hole in the wall at high speed. Someone had quick reflexes and knew how to drive." I began thinking about where the black car might be. Would people notice a filthy dinged-up car in their neighborhood? Maybe the driver dropped it off at a body shop somewhere. I wondered if Fishburn was checking out the body shops. The biggest question on my mind was, did someone ruin his car in order to put the rink out of business or did someone aim to take out Mr. Portello?

We decided to break for lunch. I remembered seeing a shady park down the street. We had each packed a lunch since we were not familiar with restaurant choices in the area. Alicia brought extra of everything because Kyle typically packed very little food.

The park offered us shade trees, picnic tables and benches, restrooms and a whisper of a breeze that knocked the temperature down one small notch.

Kyle pulled a soggy lemon grass and red ginger wrap out of his backpack.

Always the mom, Alicia pushed a bean burrito his way.

"Thanks, Allie. My lunch got squished into my psych book." He pulled the book out and wiped it off with his napkin.

Alicia turned to me. "Jo, I almost forgot to tell you

that I kind of know Mario's wife. Last night, after the ten o'clock news, Ernie and I were talking about Mr. Portello and Gianna. She retired from UCSC and we attended her retirement party two years ago. She taught biology and she subbed for Ernie at the college a few times."

"We should pay her a visit ... once she's over the shock, of course. Don't look at me like that, Allie. I just want to console her."

"You could send a card."

The afternoon painting was difficult for me. My mind kept wandering back to Mr. Portello. What kind of person was he? If someone had set out to harm him, why did that person hate him so much? Did he have a family besides his wife? Friends? Ralph didn't sound very broken up when he called.

Just as Fishburn had predicted, the clean-up crew arrived around two in the afternoon—at the height of the heat wave. I decided I needed a drink of water and toddled over to the fountain. A tall blond fellow turned around to face me.

"Josephine, what brings you ... oh, I see you're painting again," my old friend chuckled. He was half my age and built like Tarzan.

I splashed some water at my face and neck. "Chester, it's nice to see you." I splashed more water. "Looks like you have a lot to do here." I pointed to the mess.

"How 'bout I turn on the AC?" He held his smile in check.

"The AC, ah, sure, that would be nice." I felt like a fool. Why hadn't I thought of that? I cranked my head around, scanned the room and spied an AC contraption strapped to the rafters overhead.

Chester was looking in another direction. "I see Alicia over there, and that college kid...." he said.

Chester had worked on construction jobs with my crew and me in the past, and his eyes always followed Alicia. It never bothered her because she was a strong woman who loved her husband. She was the most "together" person I had ever known, except for David.

Handsome and retired at fifty-two, David owned the apricot orchard next door to my five acres of weeds and oaks situated in the rolling hills of Aromas. His cheating wife took off with the preacher ten years ago, making him perfectly available. Our friendship was growing, but I was not in a hurry to put it in writing. My husband was run over by an eighteen-wheeler sixteen years ago. I was pretty much over losing him, but I was still trying to prove to myself that Wildbrush Murals was a success and I could take care of myself.

I took care of myself, but I didn't live in my little adobe house alone. Solow, my sweet and faithful basset, was good company. Whenever I became a little unhinged or couldn't sleep at night, we ate ice cream together and felt better.

"Thinking about David?" Alicia asked.

"Yeah. Did you see Chester over there by the fountain?"

She grinned. "Hard to miss that swagger."

By four o'clock, we had had enough of the heat. The big boxy air conditioner perched in the rafters turned out to be a noisy, ineffective, glorified fan from the dark ages. I washed brushes while Alicia and Kyle loaded all the paint and equipment into my ten-year-old red Mazda pickup fitted with an invaluable red metal top that hinged over the bed.

The trip home was pleasant enough, AC on, Ray Charles singing—what more could a person want? I wanted answers to some questions, like, is someone going to come back and have another try at destroying Ralph's Rink?

CHAPTER TWO

Friday morning was a stunner. Our usual morning fog was nowhere in sight and David called to wish me a good day of painting at the rink. I didn't tell him how hot and miserable it was to work there. I just hoped and prayed the weather would be cooler.

After a refreshing shower, I slipped on a tank top and shorts, gave Solow his kibble and searched the fridge for breakfast ideas. Finally, I dumped milk, yogurt and a banana into the blender for a quick liquid meal.

Solow slapped his tail on the front porch boards as I said goodbye and hopped into my truck. He came to me three years ago through a friend who rescued dogs. She thought Solow would be a good friend and protector for me, and she was so right. He came with wonderful manners and liked my home so much I never had to worry about fencing him in. He would never leave as long as there was food around. And I loved him dearly. Sometimes I wished my feelings for David were as uncomplicated.

When I arrived at the roller rink, Alicia's Volvo and Kyle's motorcycle were already parked in the lot, not to mention Chester's Ford 350 with extra big tires, mega tool boxes and chrome everything. My painters sat under a young acacia tree, the only shade on the block. They saw me and ambled over to my truck. I eased out of my seat.

"Jo, do you think it will be as hot as yesterday?" Alicia asked.

"We've worked under worse conditions, but if you

want a day off…."

"No, absolutely not," Alicia said, as Kyle shook his head back and forth.

"Well then, let's get this stuff inside." I lifted the metal top and everyone grabbed something to carry. Paint, ladders and tools all ended up in the hot stuffy building. I stopped to scrutinize yesterday's work. The southern wall already looked like sky with its wispy clouds. Three of the five black lines had been painted.

By noon, Kyle had finished the last two black lines, Alicia had painted two gulls in flight and I had painted the trunk of the pepper tree. In the afternoon, I began drawing the notes. Kyle and Alicia followed me, painting the bold symbols black. We were already ahead of schedule. Our original five-hour days had turned into six-hour days since construction had forced the skating business to temporarily shut down.

At four o'clock, we hauled everything back to the truck. Alicia and Kyle left. I started my engine just as a shiny new BMW with custom chrome rims that reminded me of a five-point starfish pulled in beside me. It was the owner Ralph and a blond I guessed was his wife. I cut the engine and climbed out of the truck. The three of us stood together like awkward teens, not knowing the right things to say. Finally, Ralph introduced his wife and I followed the couple into the building.

Ralph and Ashley didn't even notice the partially painted mural. Their eyes were trained on the far wall, the sickening reality of destruction and death.

I decided to skip the small talk, like, "How was your vacation in Hawaii?"

Ashley popped her gum while Ralph nervously wiped sweat from his brow.

I told them what happened exactly as I saw it, excused myself and headed for home. On the way, I decided to pick up a few groceries at the market in Watsonville.

My young grocer friend, Robert, saw me coming down the produce aisle.

"Josephine, did you hear about the hit-and-run in Santa ...?"

"As a matter of fact, my current mural job happens to be at the roller rink."

Robert's jaw dropped. "Were you there when the geezer hit the gas pedal?"

"I was there, but I don't think it was a geezer. I think the whole thing was intentional." I dropped a stalk of celery and a couple artichokes into my shopping cart.

"So you're saying you think it was murder," he whispered.

"Might be, but I'm the only one who thinks so." I fingered the pears and bagged a few. The carrots looked old. My mind went to potatoes.

"Are you still painting there?" Robert asked, biting his lip as if he were looking at the gruesome scene. His freckled face quickly relaxed when he pointed to a special on strawberries.

"Any sales on Rocky Road ice cream?" Solow and I were going through Rocky Road like beer at Oktoberfest. Robert pointed to a good sale on apples, but I was already heading for the freezer aisle. I dumped half a gallon of Rocky Road in the cart and pushed on to the check out.

Wearing a blue apron too small for his chunky body, Robert greeted me at the register. He took his job very seriously, but the reason I always chose his lane was because he liked to talk about the news. He was usually a fountain of information, regurgitating all sorts of local news.

"Robert, what do you know about the roller rink, the owner in particular?"

"Ralph bought the place about five years ago from the now deceased, Mario Portello. Ralph is married to Ashley who is a friend of my mother's." Robert began bagging my groceries. "They live next door to my mom."

"Did you ever skate at the rink?"

"Does my dog have fleas? Of course, I did. Do you remember the Hokey Pokey?" He laughed. At times, Robert was a one-man grocery operation, especially when business was slow. He took my money and carried my two bags to the truck.

We laughed out loud, sharing our roller-skating stories.

Robert wished me luck with the mural, and I drove home with Ralph and Ashley tickling my mind. They had been very upset about the damage to their building. Why hadn't they expressed any emotion over Mario's sudden death?

I drove up my long gravel driveway and cut the engine. Dust billowed from behind the house, moving to my right as motor noise increased. Like the Lone Ranger riding Silver, David bumped across my field of dry weeds on his new tractor-mower. He circled each oak tree, kicking up a dust storm.

Solow lay on the front porch looking inconvenienced and out of sorts. He didn't even look up until I was standing on the porch with two bags of groceries in my arms. Food always impressed Solow. He thumped his tail, stretched and followed me into the house.

I had just finished putting the groceries away when the motor noise quit.

A minute later, David was hugging me with sweaty arms. I didn't mind since I had been working hard in the heat myself. In fact, I wanted the hug to last all night.

The phone rang. I answered it after about ten rings.

Only Mom would let it ring that long. She sounded tired.

"Mom, are you OK?"

"I would be if the weather would cool down. The heat takes all my energy. Bob's barbequing tonight, thank goodness. He said to say hello to his baby girl."

"His fifty-year-old baby girl says hi."

"Honey, are you all right? I read about the hit-and-run. I hope you still have your job," she sighed.

"Don't worry, Mom; we're painting the mural and putting up with the heat. The place has no real air conditioning. Can you believe it?" Of course, my house didn't have any either. I opened windows and doors as we talked.

"Dear, is it true that someone died in the accident?"

"Yes, it's true. Mr. Portello was sitting at his desk when the car struck, but it was no accident." Instantly, I knew I had said too much.

"The paper said it was an accident, and for once I think you shouldn't contradict the professionals." Mom sounded irritated. She said she had to go help Dad in the back yard, and hung up.

David sat across the room with a magazine on his lap pretending not to listen to my conversation with Mom. He looked up when I said I thought the police were clueless. He usually sided with my mother on such things, and this was no exception. After she hung up, he told me that Leola was right and I should let the police sort it out. He said it was not my job to get involved.

I listened and smiled. What made David think I would get involved in a hit-and-run murder?

"Josie, I'm going home to take a shower. Would you like to eat at the Grill tonight?"

"I would love to. It's too hot to cook ... and thanks for mowing ... see you later."

David hopped on his mowing machine and drove it

across my back yard, over to his. An hour later, he was back with the Miata, a clean shave and his usual well-dressed but casual good looks.

My "look" had not been as easy. I had spent most of the hour showering and primping. I came to the front door wearing a white silk blouse, black mini skirt and three-inch heels. My auburn shoulder-length hair was shiny-clean and pulled jauntily to one side. I opened the door.

"Josie, you look beautiful."

"You look pretty gorgeous yourself," I said as we embraced. I tossed Solow a doggie treat and closed the door.

"Hey, Josie, why don't we take him with us? It's a warm night. Wouldn't it be nice to eat on the patio?"

"That sounds wonderful. I hate leaving Solow all the time."

I loved having Solow on leash at our table on the patio. Our waitress loved him right away and tossed him a tortilla chip. Juanita would be his friend forever.

An elderly couple that had finished their meal stepped outside onto the patio and walked up to Solow. The old man reached into his little box of leftovers and tossed my dog a bite of steak. I think I saw Solow smile, or else it was gas. Whatever it was, it was love at first sight. The gentleman leaned closer and gave him a pat on the head.

The woman giggled.

"Tom," David said.

The man looked up. "David, haven't seen you in a coon's age, you old dog. Who's the pretty lady?"

"Tom, this is Josephine Stuart, my next door neighbor."

"Josie, I'd like you to meet my boss from IBM, Tom Trippy and his wife Lois." We stood and shook hands. "You folks still living in Prunedale?"

"Oh yeah, God's little acre. We love it there," Lois giggled, and her neck jiggled.

"What's your line of work, Josephine?" Tom asked.

"I paint murals. Currently I'm working at Ralph's Roller Rink in Santa ...."

"I saw the old rink in the news. What a mess," Tom said, lowering himself into an empty chair.

"Mr. Portello died, all because of a senior citizen," Lois sighed, and took the chair beside Tom.

"Don't believe everything you read in the paper, Lois. I was there when it happened."

"You poor dear!" she said, biting her lower lip.

"I don't know who did it, but no senior citizen can drive like the maniac I saw."

"You know," Tom said, "I helped build that roller rink almost sixty years ago when I was a college student. The place is old but I guess the steel partitions in the restrooms are still strong."

Lois giggled nervously.

"After the building was finished and inspected, the owner had us carpenters dig an underground tunnel, and then we built a couple rooms down there. Mr. Portello had us move some furniture into the place and when that was done, we reworked the floor leaving just one little trap door to get down there. You can bet your life that tunnel was never inspected. That was about fifty years before Ralph bought the place." Tom shook his head slowly, remembering the strange project.

Mr. Trippy kept us entertained with his stories and Lois with her well placed giggles as we ate our dinner. The sunset sky turned to dusk as warm breezes cooled.

Juanita flipped on patio lights and heaters, and brought us dessert menus.

David ordered four decadent desserts and the stories continued. Lois began to look tired, missing giggle opportunities here and there. But Tom had no trouble finding old stories to tell. When the four of us finally parted, it was by the light from a sliver of moon.

CHAPTER THREE

Saturday morning brought great opportunity for sleeping in, thinking, planning and housecleaning. None of that appealed to me so I dressed and treated myself to a scrumptious breakfast, which I shared with Solow. Our waistlines would suffer, but I made a mental note to have salad for lunch and ration Solow's kibble.

Mom called as I filled the dishwasher with breakfast dishes. She asked if David and I wanted to come over for dinner.

"I think we're available."

"That would be lovely, dear. Your father will be burning our dinner on the barbeque early, around six o'clock tonight."

"So we should be there by six?"

"Six would be lovely," she said, sounding like she was still suffering from the heat. Mom and Dad were a couple candles short of eighty, but in good health and more energetic than most fifty-year-olds.

There was a knock on the back door. I opened it.

"What's the matter, Josie? You look worried," David said between kisses.

"Just finished talking to Mom ... the heat really affects her, but I think she's all right. Are you available for dinner with the folks tonight?"

"As long as you're there, I wouldn't miss it," he said, rubbing Solow's ears.

"I'm going to catch up on some things around the house today. You can pick me up at five and bring some of your homemade salsa. Mom loves it." I hoped I wasn't being too short with David, but I really wanted to check out the Trippys by myself. I had already found their number in the phone book and arranged a visit.

David agreed to bring salsa and meet me at five.

I watched him walk across my newly cut weeds toward his back yard, resisting the urge to call him back. As soon as David was out of sight, I clipped a leash on Solow's collar, grabbed my purse and drove ten miles of back roads to Prunedale.

Solow had his head, neck and chest out the window, ears flying. I cranked up the music, sending him into howling ecstasy.

The town of Prunedale was ten times bigger than Aromas, but small compared to almost any town in the world. I made a right onto Langley Gulch Road.

Solow showed his approval with another high note— as high as a basset can go.

I slowed the truck, checking mailboxes for 555. I finally found the right number and headed up a steep concrete driveway. The drive circled a giant oak tree at the top of the ridge. A large house peeked out from behind acres of oaks and rolling lawns. This was real lawn, not mowed weeds. The sprawling one-story building featured large windows and panoramic views of Prunedale, the hills and a tiny glimpse of the Pacific Ocean.

I helped Solow out of the passenger seat and clipped the leash to his collar. We marched across the driveway and up half a dozen wide steps to the front door. One of the two heavy mahogany doors opened before I had time to knock. Tom and Lois stood in the doorway smiling as if the Queen was coming for tea. If I was the Queen, Solow was the King. Every move he made brought giggles from Lois and ear rubs from Tom. I looked around for signs of a dog or cat. Nothing. The elegant but "stuck in the eighties" front room looked like it had never been used by anyone for anything. I almost expected to see clear plastic covers on the matching mauve sofas.

"Lois, do you have a dog ... or maybe a cat?"

She giggled and pushed a silver curl away from her puffy round face. "Oh no, we travel too much. When we're too old to travel, we plan to get a bird."

"I just wondered. You love Solow so much...."

"We enjoy other people's pets and grandchildren," Tom said. "We have our travel and hobbies." He crossed his long legs as if he were at an IBM business meeting.

"The reason I came to see you today has to do with the roller rink. Like I told you last night, I saw a black sedan crash through the outer wall, then the office wall, then back up over Mr. Portello again before it disappeared out the hole in the wall. I think it was skillful driving—and intentional."

Lois stood up like she had just remembered something, and walked out of the room.

Tom rubbed his chin. "You might be right."

"Why do you think I might be right?" I asked.

"Because not everyone liked the old man. My brother and I worked on the rink, and when that was finished, Portello had us working on the underground rooms. We worked hard all summer. He kept telling us to wait another week, wait another week for our pay. We needed the money for tuition and rent, but he kept holding out on us. Finally, we decided not go to work. Three days of that and he was begging us to come back. He paid us and we finished the job. But that's the way he treated people. He had plenty of money—he just didn't want to let go of it.

Lois entered the room carrying a dish of homemade peanut butter cookies. She set the dish on the coffee table with a giggle. "Would your dog like a cookie?"

"Thank you, Lois, he would love one."

Lois giggled and offered me a cookie. I accepted, silently vowing to work on my waistline at a later date.

"Best cookies this side of Prunedale," Tom laughed, and snatched a cookie from the plate. "She makes her own peanut butter."

"Ach, ach rah ack?" I mumbled.

Tom cocked his head to one side.

Lois giggled.

I pointed to the hallway.

"The powder room is down the hall," Lois said.

Solow followed me to the bathroom where I rinsed peanut butter out of my mouth. Once my tongue separated from my palate, I tried to console my poor dog as he smacked his jaws together over and over. We ambled back to the living room, but not before I peeked into a few rooms. When we got back, Lois tried to give me another cookie. I finally took one, put it in my pocket and told her I would save it for after dinner.

"Tom, do you know anyone who would want to kill Mr. Portello, or maybe someone who just wants to ruin the building or the business?"

Tom rubbed his chin for a moment. "Don't forget, Josephine, I knew Mario over fifty years ago. But I remember he had a younger sister … tall and pretty with blond hair and … well, that was a long time ago." He glanced at his silent wife.

"Do you remember her name?"

"Celeste … I think. Seemed to me they didn't get along," she said.

"If you think of anyone else, please call me." I stood up, handed Tom my business card and followed Solow to the front door. Tom gave me a bear hug I wasn't expecting, and Lois gave me cookies wrapped in a paper napkin. I put the cookies where they belonged when I got home—in the garbage can.

I opened a couple windows, dropped a pile of dirty clothes in the washing machine and played my phone messages. Mom had called. She wanted me to bring dessert. I looked at the bundle of peanut butter cookies on top of the trash, and then at Solow lying on the floor smacking his lips, still trying to remove the oily peanut residue.

Feeling very domestic, I stirred up a batch of brownies. By the time I put them in the oven to bake, it was mid-afternoon and the house was uncomfortably warm. It was the fifth day of our hot spell and heat from the oven wasn't helping. Very few houses on the northern coast had air conditioning because hot weather was a rarity. I opened a couple more windows and squirted Solow and myself with cold water.

I had a half hour to kill before the brownies were done so I took Solow for a walk. He sniffed his way up Otis Road, stopping here and there to double-sniff wherever an interesting animal had passed. I was thankful for the oaks lining one side of the road, providing shade. But even with shade, we were heating up and slowing down.

Solow stopped and turned to go home.

"OK, old boy, we'll head back." I checked my watch. I had ten minutes to get home and pull the brownies out of the oven ... plenty of time. We rounded the last turn and trudged up the driveway.

I heard a meow.

Suddenly, a white fluffy-blur streaked across the driveway in front of us.

Solow howled mournfully and leaped in Fluffy's direction with great enthusiasm. His leash slipped through my fingers as he took off at basset-speed.

Fluffy flew across the dry grass.

Solow followed at a bow-legged gallop.

Fluffy rounded the tool shed behind the house with

Solow close behind. She jumped onto the remnants of a decrepit old fence.

Solow squeezed through the fence, but his leash caught on a rusty nail.

Fluffy jumped down, waved her substantial tail in the air and slowly walked toward David's house.

Solow looked at me for help. As soon as I unhooked the end of the leash, he turned and squeezed himself through a space where boards had rotted away. He galloped up to the snooty cat that stopped walking and refused to be chased.

I felt sorry for Solow. He looked like Charlie Brown when Lucy pulls the football away for the millionth time.

As I crossed the field to the house, I heard a familiar high-pitched shrieking noise. Not a siren, but close to it. It was the sound one generally hears just before the fire engines roar up to the house ... or when I'm cooking. I entered the kitchen through the back door where black smelly smoke from the oven and ear-splitting noise from the smoke detector had me gagging. I quickly turned the oven off, pulled the door open and tossed the black brownies out the back door. I opened every window and door and then followed the burnt brownies to the patio.

David and Solow joined me. Tail tucked, Solow leaned into my calves, probably wondering why I burnt the brownies. David wondered too but didn't say much. His knowing smile said it all. He happened to be a very good cook and baker because he followed directions meticulously. My methods included a certain amount of experimentation and came across as mysterious to people like my mother.

The alarm ended just as I decided I would have to kill it with a hammer. We entered the kitchen and sat down at the table.

David picked up the morning paper. "Josie, honey, I hope that wasn't anything important in the oven."

"It was our dessert to take to Mom and Dad's tonight. Don't worry about it."

He looked up at the clock on the wall. "It's only three. I can whip up a little dessert before five." He left the newspaper on the table and headed out the door. I didn't try to stop him even though I wanted to. David would garner attention for his culinary masterpiece, while Mom wondered why my baking projects seldom panned out. I consoled myself with the thought that the brownies would have been fabulous had they survived.

I finished up a few chores around the house and then went to work on myself. I tried on several outfits hoping to accomplish a casual but sensational look. I ended up with comfort as my biggest accomplishment. I dressed it up with pearl earrings and a bracelet.

I heard a knock at the front door. It was David, right on time and looking very fine in Dockers and a tan button-down shirt. He gave me a long look and a longer kiss. Solow was greeted with a couple pats on his butt. Unfortunately, Solow would have to stay home because Mom didn't like dog hairs in her house even though she told me once about the cocker spaniel her father gave her seventy years ago when she was eight-years-old. She remembered it clearly. I remember the love in her voice.

We said goodbye to Solow and climbed into David's Miata that smelled like freshly baked carrot cake. The foil-wrapped cake was out of reach in the back seat. My stomach growled as my mind wandered back there.

Mom and Dad thought the cake was delicious and praised David until my ears shriveled. Even their neighbor and dinner guest, Myrtle, said it was the best she had ever tasted. But Myrtle thought Twinkies were the best thing in the world next to fried butter. Her rhubarb pies made my face wrinkle and her bread pudding gave me heartburn.

"Josephine, I hear from your mother that you're working at the roller rink," Myrtle said, looking like the 'dough boy' squeezed into a black pantsuit, yellow scarf to hide a second chin, topped off with a curly black wig. She reminded me of an elderly bumblebee.

"Yes, we're painting the music to the Hokey Pokey."

Myrtle grinned. "Those were the days."

I glanced at her plump ankles and tried to imagine her wearing skates.

"Your mother and I used to do the Hokey Pokey," Dad laughed.

Mom smiled. "We still love to skate. Your father is very graceful on...."

"Your mother and father rolled by my house on rollerblades yesterday. Some people never age," Myrtle said as she shuffled across the floor gingerly carrying two empty dessert plates to the kitchen.

Mom and I cleared the rest of the table.

"Poor Mario," Myrtle sighed, "minding his own business, and, bam, he's run down by some oldster. Why are you shaking your head, Josephine?"

"I don't believe it was an oldster; the driving was very well done—intentional, I think. I'm wondering who hated him that much." We all moved into the living room.

"Mario was close to my age and a very private person," Myrtle said, "but his younger sister was the life of every party. Celeste loved to have fun. We went to Girl Scout Camp together; and she kept the place in stitches, made the homesick girls forget about home. Leola, do you remember Celeste Portello?"

"I do," Bob cleared his throat. "Very interesting girl."

Mom gave him a look that would frost a hot poker.

Myrtle seemed to be walking down memory lane. She remembered Mario letting certain pretty girls use the rental skates for free. There was a rumor that he loaned money to people who needed it, and he gave heavily to the Catholic Church.

CHAPTER FOUR

Because Aromas was wrapped in thick fog, Sunday morning was perfect for sleeping late. My bedroom stayed dark, and the normal bird concert outside my window didn't happen because birds are not cheerful when they are cold and wet. I was warm and comfy under the blankets until loud banging on the front door began. I pulled on my robe, hurried through the house, peeked out the living room window and laughed until I cried.

"Thanks, Josie; I thought you would never let me in," David groaned. He wore blue boxers and a silly smile. He looked at my laughing eyes and said, "I accidentally locked myself out of the house when I went for the newspaper."

Solow leaned against David's bare calves, probably feeling sorry for his shivering friend holding a newspaper in one hand.

"This whole lock-your-door thing is ridiculous," I said. "I know there were a couple of burglaries in Aromas, but who's going to come out here and what would they take? My TV is ancient, my computer barely runs and I don't even own a spindle … nimble … kindle thingy."

"Hey, the sheriff's department put out a warning, and they want everyone to lock their doors." David shrugged, sat down on the sofa and pulled a pink lap blanket over his long legs. He had "Tom Selleck legs," chocolate-colored eyes and a head of thick salt and pepper hair. He was in good shape for a fifty-two-year-old retired IBM executive.

"David, I don't even know if I have a key to your house anymore. What about the key you put under the potted geranium on the back patio?"

"You have it, don't you remember?"

"Oh, yeah; I'll look for it." I walked to the kitchen to be alone for a moment, to think. After pressuring my brain to give up the key, it finally reminded me that I had been wearing my white windbreaker the day I needed a cup of sugar and David wasn't home. I went to the coat closet, checked the windbreaker pockets, retrieved the key and handed it over to the guy with the "I told you so" smile.

An hour later, David left. My smile didn't fade until the phone rang. It was Alicia.

"Hi, Allie; what's up?"

"Wow, Jo, you sound perky."

"David just left...."

"Oh, I see."

"He was locked out of his house ... so I found the key, and we spent some time together ... that's all." My cheeks were hot. I knew Alicia was holding back a giggle. I shared all kinds of information with her, but not about my private time with David.

"Have you read the newspaper yet?" she asked.

"No, I've been ... busy."

"Well, on page two, it shows a picture of the rink, the inside that is, over by the freezer and water fountain. It seems they found germs in the water fountain and mouse droppings near the freezer. I'm afraid the rink is getting a bad reputation with the public."

"So the health department is worried about mice getting in the freezer and eating the popsicles?"

"Who knows?" she said. "I think someone's after Ralph's business."

"You mean the new outdoor rink on the west side?"

"Maybe. I'll talk to you later, Jo. I have to make breakfast for the boys." She hung up.

I lumbered over to the fridge to see what would inspire me. Eventually, I amassed ingredients for a Denver omelet, fried it and shared it with Solow. I cleaned the kitchen, showered and dressed. By that time, it was ten o'clock. I called Alicia to see if she wanted to go to Santa Cruz with me.

"Sure, Jo, I'll go with you; and yes, I would like to see the outdoor rink."

"Ok, pick you up in half an hour." We hung up.

One look at Solow and I knew he knew I was leaving him again. Eyes just don't get any sadder than his. He followed me around the house as I gathered up my windbreaker, purse and keys. I gave him a last ear-rub and shut the door. A mournful howl reverberated through the oak panels, stabbing into my heart.

I put my truck into drive, turned up the radio and roared twelve miles down the road to the Quintana's lovely two-story home at the edge of Drew Lake in Watsonville. Alicia explained that Ernie had taken Trigger to a golf lesson as she piled into my truck the instant it stopped moving. She looked very well put-together in designer jeans and white peasant blouse with loopy silver earrings and a silver and turquoise necklace. I told her I planned to stop at the roller rink first.

We headed north on Highway One to the east side of Santa Cruz. I parked in front of Ralph's Roller Rink. We climbed out of the truck and ducked under yellow tape stretched across a gaping hole in the wall.

An ear-splitting saw suddenly went quiet.

"Hey, you can't come in here … oh, Josephine, Alicia, what are you two doing here?" Chester asked. Obviously, he and another carpenter were working on a Sunday, trying to get the rink up and running again.

Most of the debris had been removed from the building, except for a pile of old green carpet where the office used to be.

"Did you see the paper this morning?" I asked Chester, as he stuffed his thumbs in his back pockets.

"No, I was here pretty early. It was still dark...." His eyes went to Alicia.

"If the county health department gets their way, this place might be closed longer than we thought," I said, looking at the water fountain, wishing I had never used it. "The health department found germs and mouse droppings."

Chester shook his head and laughed. "Is this a rink or a restaurant? It's probably old man Waller. He's good at shutting people down, especially when he doesn't like them."

I walked across the floor where the office used to be. At that point, it was open hardwood flooring with a pile of old green carpet in the middle of the room. I noticed that the office had shared a wall with the ladies' restroom. The sturdy stall had stopped the car in its tracks. The metal was slightly dented, just a flesh wound, really. It was just lucky that the rink wasn't open for business when the car smashed through the walls, or was that part of someone's plan?

I wandered over to the north wall where three six-foot-high shelves full of skates for rent stood shoulder-to-shoulder. I went behind the counter, ignoring Chester's worried looks, as I snooped around just for the fun of it. The wood floor between the wall and the counter was cluttered with various unattractive rugs—some large, some small.

Alicia pestered me to leave things alone.

I didn't know what I was looking for; I was just looking. I reached up to a top shelf and pulled down a pair of skates that would have fit a four-year-old.

"Aren't these the cutest ... oops!" A glass jar of tootsie pops teetered and fell six feet to the floor, smashing into bits. In that short moment of tootsie-trouble, I remembered that the winner of the limbo dance was always treated to a free tootsie pop.

I looked around. No one was smiling. Alicia pursed her lips and Chester quickly zipped over to his hole-in-the-wall construction job.

I put the skates back, crouched down on my haunches and began separating wrapped candy from pieces of glass with Alicia's help. I noticed a large ornate key in the pile of candy and slipped it into my pocket, planning to put it in a new jar. We put the candy on the counter, and I shook glass out of the rug.

Alicia shook the rug again and swept up the glass.

When the floor was clean, I spread the rug in its usual place.

"Jo, are you finished here?" Alicia asked.

"Sure. Allie, remind me to shop for a glass jar today and fill it with the candy tomorrow."

She rolled her eyes to the ceiling, opened her mouth to speak, but chuckled instead.

I finally remembered what I had wanted to see for myself, the freezer. I bent down and looked closely for mouse droppings in and on the appliance. Either someone had recently cleaned the area, or the health department made a mistake. However, there was an official looking pink slip signed by James Waller taped to the freezer door. Was that the Waller in the newspaper who said he might run for Mayor?

Alicia and I said goodbye to Chester and high-tailed it to my truck for a short ride across town to the outdoor rink on the west side. We found the rink and skateboard park in a redeveloped industrial area near the railroad tracks. Industry and the train had left Santa Cruz years ago, giving the good-time folks more room to play. The fair-weather rink was about the same size as Ralph's place, but it had a concrete floor and no walls. The skateboard park and skating rink were free to the public, except for the food.

We watched a dozen or so experienced skaters streaking around the rink on rollerblades and another group of youngsters plodding along, barely able to stand up on their own skates. The rules were posted on the wall of the snack shack. Every skater must wear kneepads and a helmet. The shack was open for business so we decided to buy some lunch.

"This must be where Kyle buys his lunch." I read the menu board out loud. "Bean curd and lemon grass wrap, hazelnut-lime espresso, pine nut ice cream bar, kelp and guanabana berry smoothie ... I don't think I'm hungry."

"It's those high prices that scare me," Alicia said, holding her throat.

Minutes later, I parked my truck in front of the local Denny's on Ocean Street. No guanabana berries, just old-fashioned food for old-fashioned appetites. We followed the greeter toward a table in the far corner, located just past a table of older men all wearing shiny gold shirts. I knew most of them. They were pillars of the church in the morning and bowling champions in the afternoon.

Dad stood up for a hug. A tall heavy-set gentleman wearing bifocals and a gold shirt pulled a chair out for Alicia and another for me.

"Jim Waller at your service," the overly smiley fellow said.

Dad introduced everyone to Alicia. "Don't mind Jim. He thinks he's already mayor." Everyone laughed.

I sat next to Dad, admiring his willpower, having soup for lunch—until the banana split arrived. By that time, Alicia and I were halfway through our sandwiches, and Mr. Waller was still sharing his pointless stories.

Finally, the men got up to leave, picking up their bill and ours. Dad said they had a game at the Bowl and Bowl at 2:30. As they walked away, I wished them luck.

"Allie, what did you think of Mr. Waller?"

"He should be on a diet, his stories were boring, but other than that...."

"I think he's the guy Chester was talking about—the guy who works for the health department. Jim could be James."

"Maybe," Alicia said, "but he's kind of old to be a health inspector."

"Sounds like he plans to retire right into the mayor business."

We stopped at my cousin Candy's florist shop just three blocks from Denny's and bought a glass jar similar to the one that broke. I put it behind the front seat for safekeeping, dropped Alicia at her house and went on home. I was looking forward to a relaxing afternoon and evening with David and Solow.

Through the dusty windshield, I saw a note taped to my front door.

I climbed out of the truck and walked up to the message, instantly recognizing David's handwriting. He explained that he had to go to Modesto to take care of his little granddaughter, Monica. Harley had an appointment out of town, insurance business, and the sitter wasn't available. Maybe it was a good thing. Maybe David and I would tire of each other if we were always together. But I was not tired of him yet—in fact, I missed him.

I felt something touch my ankle and whirled around. Soft purring began as big blue-green eyes stared up at me. The tiny, grungy yellow ball of matted fur meowed.

I bent down, picked the little fellow up and cuddled him.

Solow howled from inside the house.

Sharp claws dug into my hands.

I dropped the critter on the porch, unlocked the front door and went inside, figuring the kitten would go back to wherever it came from.

Solow sniffed me up and down as if I had not been true to him. He pointed his nose at the door and let out a quick bark.

"You need to go out?" I opened the door and he ran up to the little yellow menace. They touched and sniffed. I had the feeling Solow wanted to have a good chase, but this little guy wasn't going anywhere.

Hours passed as I cleaned house, laundry and the back patio. Solow circled the house and found me sunning myself on the patio. Half a minute later, the kitten rounded the house and attacked Solow's leg, batting it with his little paw. Solow stiffened and looked up at me for help when the cat leaped onto his tail, lost his grip and slid to the ground. Solow tried to get away, but the gutsy little fellow was back on his trail like nuts on a sundae.

CHAPTER FIVE

A lick on my cheek and hot dog-breath in my face pulled me out of a lovely dream where David and I were drifting along the coast in a broken down motorboat. Dolphins wearing zebra stripes escorted us as we entered a fog bank and lost our way.

"Solow, what are you doing up so early?" I looked at the clock and then at my antsy dog. "I guess nature is calling." It was Monday, a workday, so I pushed my feet into slippers and yawned my way down the hall to the back door. Before the door was halfway open, Solow pushed his way outside where the little yellow kitten was mewing for him.

The scrawny little guy looked even skinnier than the day before. In my experience, feral cats usually find food on their own, like mice, gophers, lizards, birds and that sort of thing. I had to admit that this cat was probably too young to hunt. I scanned the dense foliage obscuring a view of Otis Road from my house, wondering if a hidden mother cat worried over her adventurous kitten.

I watched the kitten bat Solow's long ears and run figure eights around his short stocky legs. The only interaction my dog had ever had with a cat was with Fluffy who humiliated him at least once a day. Solow surprised me when he took most of the kitten's antics in his stride.

Against my better judgment, I brought out a bowl of milk for the kitten.

Solow stood back from the bowl, letting the little creature drink. He drank with enthusiasm, creating a white mustache that covered half his face. I leaned down and put my hand on his soft back. Quick as lightening, the cat squirmed around and ran claws across my hand. Three rows of little red beads appeared.

I grumbled to myself, "Should have known better," as I washed the scratches thoroughly with soap and water. "Ouch!" Solow stayed outside while I showered, dressed and ate breakfast. I poured kibble in his bowl, bribed him with a doggie biscuit to come inside and left for work.

As soon as I started my thirty-five-mile drive to Santa Cruz, I forgot all about the kitten and Solow's peculiar behavior. My thoughts turned to Mr. Portello, which reminded me of a skating party I had attended when I was about ten years old. I tried to remember who had handed me a Tootsie pop for being the best at doing the Limbo. Being naturally limber and small as a child got me the big prize. Some kids line their bedrooms with trophies—I won a Tootsie Pop.

From Tootsie Pops, my mind wandered back to lunch at Denny's and the distinguished-looking Jim Waller. Wasn't Jim short for James? Were Jim Waller and James Waller the same man? My mind was running amuck when suddenly an awkward lane-change happened and a horn blasted me back to the moment.

I rolled into town and parked between Kyle's yellow motorcycle and Alicia's Volvo.

Alicia and Kyle stood against the east wall of the roller rink where the morning sun was revving up for another hot day. As my friends helped me carry our equipment inside, they never mentioned my lateness. But they did wear smirky smiles. Alicia asked if the scratches on my hand had anything to do with my arrival time. I told her about the murderous kitten and all she could say was "aw."

Alicia and I had painted together for several years. I hired Kyle a year ago when Alicia's husband, Ernie, a professor at UCSC, recommended him. He looked like a kid and painted like a pro. Kyle worked on the music notes while Alicia added another seagull.

I went back to the truck for the candy jar. Just as I pulled it out and slammed the door, a shiny black BMW pulled to a stop.

Since I couldn't think of any excuse for being at the cash counter and breaking his jar, I pretended I didn't see Ralph and hurried inside, holding the jar in front of my body. Once I was inside, I literally ran the length of the rink, straight to the counter and scooped all the pops into the jar. There wasn't time to place it on the shelf where it belonged, so I just left it on the counter and hurried over to the ladies' restroom while Alicia chit-chatted with Ralph.

Ralph and I crossed paths as I casually strolled toward the mural wall. He wore a friendly smile and wished me a good morning.

"Good morning," I said. "Did you know that the health department was here?"

Ralph's eyes tracked across the room to the official-looking pink paper taped to the freezer. He nodded, and the smile faded. "The guy's a snoop—inspected every inch of this place."

"I heard about the violation so I looked around. I didn't see any mouse droppings," I said cheerfully.

"Maybe that was because I cleaned them up," Ralph said and walked away.

I picked up a piece of chalk and drew a few more notes for Kyle to paint. The three of us worked until noon, took our lunch break at the park and watched the hot spell come to an end. A dark grey wall of fog sat off shore. The cool breeze had become a cold wind by the time we finished lunch. I had goose bumps on top of my goose bumps. Alicia wore cut-offs like mine, and we both shivered as we fast-walked back to the rink.

Alicia and Kyle went back to work immediately.

I meandered over to the water fountain and remembered the germ report just in time. It was safer to be thirsty. I watched Chester deftly measure and cut a two-by-four for the frame of the office reconstruction. The old carpet had been hauled away, revealing an interesting pattern in the wood floor. In the center of the room, the hardwood planks stopped around an inset two-foot by two-foot plywood section with a rusty keyhole in one corner. It occurred to me that the keyhole was big like the big brass key I found in the candy jar.

I heard voices.

The front entrance door was propped open with a five-gallon bucket of paint. I noticed a silver sedan parked at the sidewalk. In between power-saw cuts of wood, I listened to the owner of the silver car as she talked to Ralph.

The woman's name was Bonnie and she owned the bingo parlor two doors down. She came by to see the damage and ask Ralph what his plans were for the rink. At that point, they walked over to the mural wall and spoke to my painters. I caught up to them and introduced myself.

Bonnie wore lots of pink; but when she spoke, her gravelly voice reminded me of Louie Armstrong. She stood at least six inches taller then me on her platform flip flops full of bling and wore beaded bracelets up and down her hairy, muscular arms. She looked close to my age, but with the heavy make-up and nose job, it was hard to tell for sure.

"Josephine," Bonnie said. "I'm sure the mural will be very interesting to look at when it's finished." Another way of saying, "It doesn't look very good so far."

"Thank you, Bonnie; nice of you to check out our work." I turned, picked up my chalk and scratched out a few more notes for Kyle to paint. I felt Bonnie's eyes on my back and her garlic breath singeing my hair.

"Did you know Mr. Portello?" I asked.

"Not personally. He was a recluse, you know what I mean?"

"So you work two doors down and never talked to him?"

"Oh, maybe a couple times ... I can't remember exactly."

Kyle worked on the musical notes just a few feet to my left. Bonnie sized him up, stepped closer to his lanky frame and batted her fake lashes at him. Kyle didn't look away from his work, sensing Bonnie was close by. The garlic scent was probably a strong clue. His face turned ripe tomato red, which put a smile on the homely woman's face. Looking satisfied, she turned and sashayed her broad shoulders and bony hips across the rink to the open front door, giving the hips an extra swing as she passed by the carpenters.

I had the feeling Bonnie would flirt with a sack of potatoes if that was all she could find. She didn't seem to be broken up about the death of Mario—actually, no one seemed to care very much. Ashley hadn't shown any emotion for the man, only for the damage to the building, and Ralph only worried about reopening the rink as soon as possible. I felt sad for Mario, even though I hadn't known him.

Kyle had several notes to work on so I decided to slip out the back door for some air. I wandered through the parking lot to the two-story lavender stucco building two doors down, where Bonnie did her bingo business. I peeked into a trashcan labeled "recycle."

It was full to the brim with smashed Dr. Pepper cans.

A gravelly voice asked what I was looking for.

My red face popped up. I looked into Bonnie's dark eyes.

"I ... ah, wanted to throw my gum wrapper away."

"Don't put it in that one. Here, this one's for trash." She held the lid up while I made a fist and pretended to drop a wad of paper in the can.

Bonnie looked at me funny but didn't say anything.

"Did Mario have any friends?" I asked.

"You're really on a Mario kick, aren't you? Was he your evil godfather or something?" She held her head high, looking through heavy lashes at half-mast.

"It's getting chilly out here," I said. "I think I'll go back to work. See ya."

Bonnie waved a couple fingers, turned and entered her building from the back door.

I walked up to Alicia to see how the birds were coming along. The building was unusually quiet because all the usual people had already left. It was almost four, time to clean up and head home. My dedicated painters were ready. While I was away, they had cleaned up and packed up everything. Two trips to the truck and we were ready to lock the door and head home.

I waved to Alicia and Kyle as they drove away and reentered the building to make a last minute inspection, my one chance to look around without having to explain why to anyone. The cavernous interior smelled like a combination of old wood and Chester's freshly cut new wood. I inspected the two-by-four wall frames destined to become the new office. All they needed was wallboard, electrical outlets, paint, a door and carpet.

I walked around the inside of the unfinished room that shared a wall with the ladies' restroom. Was that a fly on the wall? I leaned closer for a better look. A small hole had been drilled into the restroom wall. It happened to be at my eye-level. I squeezed between the two-by-fours, circled around to the restroom door and entered.

Concrete floor, a couple long wooden benches, three stalls and two sinks, and nothing had been up-graded in at least forty years. The room reminded me of my skating days as a child. I entered one stall, nothing unusual, just busy flower wallpaper with phone numbers written in lipstick. After searching the second stall carefully, I found a small hole in the wall at my eye-level. The hole was not easy to see because it disappeared into the wallpaper pattern—little faded flowers with bumblebees checking for honey. One bumblebee had a hole in his body if you looked very closely.

I peeked through the hole, right into the newly framed office.

All the way home I asked myself the question, "Was the hole intentional?" Maybe it had held a fixture to the wall or a picture. Finally I stopped obsessing over the hole and decided to pick up some fast food for dinner. I was already in Aromas when the food idea struck, so I stopped at Marshall's Grocery and bought a burrito. It smelled so good I decided to have a bite or two while I drove.

Solow greeted me at the front porch, his tail wagging his whole body. He smelled the last bite of my burrito, so I tossed it to him. The large bite flew down his throat without benefit of tasting or chewing.

I checked my phone messages and emails. Alicia had sent an email containing Mrs. Portello's address and phone number. I never liked to pressure my friends for favors, but my pleading had worked. Alicia usually went along with my ideas, but she was slow to get on board with the idea that Mario had been murdered. But since I was the only eyewitness to the hit-and-run, she almost had to believe me.

I heard a rap on the front door and opened it. David was back in town, smiling like a Cheshire cat, waving a pizza box in front of me. The pesto-chicken smell lulled me into thinking I was a tad-bit hungry. We ate pizza until my burrito screamed, "Enough!"

"What's the matter, Josie? Don't you like the pizza?"

"I love the pizza … it's the burrito I'm worried about."

"Oh."

CHAPTER SIX

Tuesday morning I was up before the alarm clock had a chance to startle me into consciousness. I woke up because Solow had his wet nose touching my cheek. His doggie breath had me dreaming about four-legged drooling seagulls at the county dump.

I pushed Solow away and closed my eyes.

He lifted his head and let out a mournful howl.

"Ok, I'm up. What is your problem?" I pulled on a robe and escorted Solow to the back door. He stood in the doorway, not in, not out and refused to move. "What's going on with you? Wait ... I hear something, like a meow." I looked past the patio to the giant mass of wild lilac bushes conveniently hiding my house from traffic on Otis Drive. I listened. There was another meow. I followed Solow across the patio and through a short stretch of dry weeds to a drainage ditch half covered by lilac branches, better known as "tick bushes."

Solow stepped down into the ditch and pushed his way through the flowering branches.

He stopped and looked up at me for help.

I put one lovely snowball slipper into the ditch and then the other, bent down and picked up a filthy, bloody kitten that weighed less than a small kitten should weigh. It opened its mouth to meow, but hardly a squeak came out. The little eyelids closed as I carried him in one hand back to the house. I forgot all about getting ready for work. Cleaning the leg wound and serving up a bowl of warm milk had become a priority.

The kitten was beyond struggling. It lay quietly as I

cleaned the two gashes on its hind leg. Maybe an animal had tried to make a meal of the kitten before it escaped and hid in the ditch. I didn't know exactly what happened and since I had never owned a cat before, I could only guess at how to take care of the little fellow.

Solow watched attentively as I fed the kitten a few licks of milk from my finger. I made a little nest out of a dishtowel next to the bowl of milk on the kitchen floor. I felt ribs as I put the little guy into his nest. His eyes closed and I turned my focus on a shower and breakfast. He slept through all of that.

Scary thoughts marched through my brain. What if the kitten didn't wake up and drink the milk? What if Solow drank the milk and the cat went to kitty heaven while I was at work? How could I make sure the little creature had enough to eat? That's when I thought of the turkey baster. I found it at the back end of the utensils drawer, squeezed the rubber bulb, stuck the tip into the bowl and sucked up some milk.

Solow stayed close to the kitten, watching intently as I pressed the tip of the baster to the cat's tiny mouth. The mouth wiggled but did not open.

Solow woofed softly.

The mouth fell open and milk gushed into it, and up his little pink nose. I cleaned his face. Kitty's eyes stayed closed but a pink tongue poked out, searching for more milk. I squirted little milky squirts again and again, watching the belly fill and the ribs disappear from view. His eyes were still closed when I grabbed my purse and told Solow I had to leave. Solow didn't follow me to the door. He just kept his eyes on the patient—who knew he would grow up to be a nurse?

My little red truck roared up Highway One to Ralph's Roller Rink. Like many other coastal towns, Santa Cruz was smothered in wet, gloomy fog. I parked next to Chester's pickup, climbed out of my seat and shivered.

Alicia and Kyle left the warmth of her car and joined me as I pulled supplies from the truck bed. Two trips and everything was inside. I flipped on some overhead lighting and filled a couple of quart-size containers with water from the fountain.

"Are you sure you want to use that fountain?" Chester laughed.

"Oh, didn't see you there. The water's for our brushes … and I don't believe there's anything wrong with this fountain anyway. I used it all the time when I was a kid and nothing happened to me."

"So you think the health inspector's report is bogus?" he smiled.

"If my brushes get sick I'll let you know." I had grown up as an only child; but if I could have had a brother, I would want one like Chester. I put my hand in my pocket and pulled out the key from the candy jar.

"Where did you get that old-fashioned key?" Chester asked, as he inspected it.

"My grandfather had a door key like this," I said. "I found it in the candy jar."

Chester turned his head, looking for a place to use the key.

We looked at each other and instantly knew where it belonged. I knelt down beside the section of plywood in the middle of the office floor and pushed the key into the keyhole. A perfect fit. I turned it. Dumbfounded, I pulled up on the key. The wooden square of flooring rose up with the key a couple inches. Chester put his fingers under the wood, lifted it and set it down away from the hole.

On my knees, I leaned down to inspect the opening. "Wow, dirty air. There's a ladder, but it's really dark down there." My heart pounded. I wondered if Ralph knew about the hole in the floor. Maybe this was what

Tom Trippy had been telling us about. I stood up and Chester and I high-fived each other. He looked as excited as I felt. We were the only people in the west side of the building. My painters were too far away and too busy to know that anything unusual had happened.

Chester held my wrist as I stretched my right leg a wee bit down the hole and hooked my foot onto the first rung. "You're not going down there, are you?"

I ignored his question, placed my left foot on a lower rung and started down the ladder. My hips barely squeezed through the opening. Something brushed across my face. "Eek! What was that?"

"Are you all right, Josephine?" Chester asked.

I thought of spiders—big ones. But it turned out to be a string hanging from a light bulb. I pulled on it and the bulb went bright. Once I squeezed my shoulders through the opening, and my head went below floor-level, I was looking at an underground tunnel about ten or twelve feet long, four feet wide, with a basic concrete floor and old wooden walls stretching up to the six-foot-high ceiling, obviously the underpinnings of the building.

At the end of the tunnel was a shorter-than-average door. Off to my left was a large antique metal door ensconced in the wooden wall. In the center of the five-foot door was a combination lock and handle. Before I had time to dismount from the ladder, Chester called me back in a loud whisper, telling me that Ralph had just come in the back door and was talking to Alicia.

I scampered six steps up the ladder, pulled the string to turn out the light and popped out of the hole with a helping hand from Chester. We dropped the wooden trap door into place. He went back to measuring two-by-fours; and I casually walked over to the fountain, wishing I had had more time in the tunnel. Even if Ralph knew about the tunnel, his two-hundred-pound body would have a hard time squeezing down that little rabbit-hole. Whoever used it had to be a smaller person, like Mr. Portello.

I dropped the key into my pocket.

Ralph walked straight to Chester with a question about the new office.

I picked up the two jars of water and joined my friends. I found a piece of chalk and drew a few more notes for Kyle.

My cell phone rang. It was David.

"I hate to tell you, Josie, but there's a kitten in your house...."

"Yeah, I found him this morning all beat up, lying in a ditch. Is he still alive?"

"He's alive all right. I came over to get my toolbox you borrowed, and here's this itsy bitsy cat leaping from chair to chair and then right up the drapes, and then he meows because he doesn't know how to get down. I climbed up on a chair and put him on the floor. Next thing, I look up and he's up there again. I guess the little devil will be all right."

"I think he's feral. What do you think?"

"I don't know, but he sure has a lot of energy," David laughed. "Are we still on for dinner tonight?"

"Sure, but I have some errands so let's make it seven instead of six, Ok?"

"Ok with me." We hung up.

I had found Mario's sister's address in the phone book, and I planned to use it. I had called Celeste the night before and arranged a visit. She lived on the west side of Santa Cruz, just ten minutes from the rink.

"Alicia, are you doing anything after work?"

"No, what do you have planned for me?" she asked with a one-eyed squint.

"Not much. I was just wondering if you would like to meet Celeste, sister of the dead guy ... you know,

Mr. Portello."

"Don't tell me you're looking for a murderer when no one even thinks Mario was murdered. Jo, sometimes you need to take a deep breath and relax."

"Allie, you know me pretty well. You know I'm usually right about these things, right?"

Alicia rolled her eyes to the rafters and agreed to accompany me to Celeste's place. We arrived at her apartment house a little after four. I double-checked the address. The place was turn-of-the-century gorgeous, a white stucco period piece hugging a hillside of palms, ferns and giant rhododendrons and azaleas. A dozen wide stone steps took us to a long veranda and the main entrance to The Piedmont. I found a list of names and pressed the button next to Celeste's name.

A couple minutes went by. One of the giant etched glass doors opened and a bleached blond, made up to look like Madonna, poked her head out.

"You must be Josephine," she said, looking squarely at Alicia.

"I'm Josephine and this is my friend, Alicia. You're taller than your brother," I blurted, as I took in her sparse crown of dyed golden hair controlled with a glittery sweatband.

"He was my stepbrother. He hated that I was taller. Actually, he hated everything about me. Won't you come in?" she smiled, sending deep creases up and down her shallow cheeks. She reminded me of someone who bounces from diet to diet, never feeling like they are skinny enough.

We followed Celeste across a large, high-ceilinged room featuring classic arches, a "Gone with the Wind" staircase, niches, corbels, giant gold-framed mirrors and imported rugs. In the center of the cream-colored room on a large antique coffee table sat a very substantial vase full of fresh gladiolas. I could easily imagine flappers lounging in this room when it was a hotel, wearing 1920's hats, suits and dresses. A cluster of about thirty little copper boxes, formerly mailboxes, hung on the wall as a reminder of the building's past.

"My apartment is down the hall, but we can visit here." Celeste dropped into a period piece sofa upholstered in white brocade. "What is it you would like to talk about?"

Alicia and I sat on twin Queen Ann chairs facing Celeste.

"I don't know how to say this," I began, "but I think your stepbrother was murdered. I saw the whole thing happen, and it looked intentional to me." In my mind, I had rehearsed a little "how are you doing" speech on the way over, but dropped the idea when I realized Celeste was not stuck in sorrow.

"I wouldn't be surprised if someone murdered him," she said flatly.

"Oh, what makes you think that?" I watched Alicia begin to look interested.

"There were complaints from his neighbors. You see, there was a walking path that crossed his property. He put up a fence, and all the walkers, joggers and skateboarders had to use the street. And then ... let me think ... there was something about yappy dogs. Mario wasn't the most sociable guy, if you know what I mean."

"Did you grow up in the same house with him?" Alicia asked.

"No. I was fifteen when my mom married Mario's dad. Mario was about twenty. There came a time when he fancied me, but I wasn't interested and let him know it."

"What do you think of Mario's wife? Did they get along as a couple?" I asked.

"If you call not killing each other 'getting along,'"

she cackled. "Why are you even interested, Josephine? What was my weird stepbrother to you?"

"Actually, I never met Mario. I saw him come out of his office once, but he didn't see me. It's hard to explain my feelings. The man lived his life until someone killed him. I need to find the killer—this obsession has happened to me before. I expect justice."

Alicia nodded her head, vouching for my words.

"Celeste, do you know of any confrontations, enemies, someone who might have wanted to kill your stepbrother, besides the bike path and yappy dogs?"

She stared at her bony knuckles for a moment, shaking her head slowly.

We took turns telling Celeste how sorry we were—blah, blah, blah and left The Piedmont to the well-heeled retired folks. As we drove across town to the roller rink, I shared my thoughts with Alicia. Either Mario was a horrible person and that was why he had no friends, or Mario was quiet, shy and misunderstood. Obviously, I needed another opinion on his character, but that would have to wait.

I dropped Alicia at her car behind the rink, drove home and snuggled my truck into a spot beside David's Miata. He must have heard me drive up and opened the front door. My wide-eyed date stepped outside and quickly closed the door, looking like he had been flopping around in a clothes dryer full of mint jelly. Unfortunately, he smelled more like broccoli than mint.

"What happened to you? Are you all right? Is that blood on your face?" I asked as I slammed the truck door.

"I'm going home to take a shower. Careful when you open that door." He did not explain further, just walked like a zombie past his car, down the driveway and took a right on Otis.

I cautiously opened the front door. Solow howled

three times, sounding like I had been away for days instead of hours. He leaned against my calf as we walked to the kitchen. I rounded the breakfast bar. Suddenly something landed on the back of my neck. I shook and wiggled until it fell off. I looked down at the floor in amazement.

"Oh, you poor little kitty cat." I bent down to give it a pat on the head, but yanked my hand back as blood spurted. For being half-dead in the morning, his afternoon was a circus. He scampered across the linoleum, leaped onto a chair, then onto the table, marched up to a bowl of fruit and bit into a cherry. From there, he climbed the mountain of fruit and decided to take a nap on top of my peaches.

I noticed his milk bowl was empty. I filled it, grabbed the kitten by the scruff of his neck and set him down in front of the milk. He started to walk away. I grabbed him again and pushed his nose into the milk. He licked his face and began lapping up his dinner.

Solow licked the cat's back and tail while he filled his belly.

Apparently, David had cleaned the kitten during the day because the dried blood and dirt were missing. The little guy had beautiful medium-length yellow hair, blue-green eyes and a tiny pink nose. I had always thought feral cats were afraid of people, but this one had everyone afraid of it—except Solow, who stayed close to his new little charge.

When the cat's stomach looked round enough to pop, he staggered over to the dishtowel nest on the floor and plopped down for a nap. Solow lay beside him.

I smiled, thinking my sweet basset would have made a wonderful father. I had already forgotten the scratches on my hand and down my back.

A knock on the back door reminded me that I needed to clean up and change clothes for my date with David.

I opened the door. He looked wonderful except for a scratch on his forehead.

"Feisty little guy, isn't he?" I said.

"You have no idea how feisty."

I hurried down the hall to my room for a quick change of clothes.

CHAPTER SEVEN

It was a typical Wednesday morning. I rolled out of bed and trudged down the hall, opening one eye at a time. I let Solow out the back door. The kitchen smelled wonderful, like mint, lemon, ginger, and maple syrup. Both eyes burst wide open. My favorite tea bags had been sliced, diced and dumped into a pool of real maple syrup on the floor. Mr. Kitten had his nose in the syrup, lapping it up. I would never know for sure how he managed to shove the bottle from a top shelf, but the proof was the broken glass.

"You little brat! You are the worst animal I ever met. You're going outside."

I grabbed the impudent little cat by the back of his scrawny neck and dropped him onto the patio where Solow waited, looking guilty on behalf of his friend.

"Here's your buddy Bratworse," I told Solow. I placed his bowl of milk on the patio and shut the door.

Mr. Bratworse was giving me a headache, not to mention making me late to work again. Ralph had entrusted me with the key to the building, which meant I was holding up carpenters and painters. I drove into the rink parking lot and spied two painters and two carpenters standing near the back entrance. It looked like Chester had the floor because the other three were laughing.

I parked and walked up to my friends.

Kyle greeted me. "Josephine, you never told us about the time you set off the security alarm and the sheriff's deputies...."

"That's an old story, Kyle, and Chester always

exaggerates." I unlocked the door and we filed into the empty building, each of us carrying a load of painting equipment. I thought it was rather unfair that Chester was allowed to leave his tools in the building for as long as it took to complete the job.

Once I had Alicia and Kyle working on music notes, I trotted over to the west side of the building and quickly inserted the over-sized key in the keyhole, opening the door to a mysterious underground space where my imagination clicked into overdrive. I already knew how to turn on the light, and quickly found the string. My right foot touched the concrete floor, then the left foot found purchase.

The air smelled of old timbers, earth, rot and chemicals I could not identify.

"Hey, Josephine, are you at it again?" Chester shouted down the hole.

"Shhhhh! I'm just going to take a quick look around," I said, knowing that Alicia would disapprove. I moved away from the ladder and the light source, to the door at the end of the hall. It stood slightly ajar, tempting me to enter. Hinges squeaked when I pushed it open, sending prickles up my body. I ducked my head and entered the dark little room. I groped around for a light switch, found one on the wall, flipped it and a pair of two-foot overhead fluorescent bulbs slowly burst into bright light.

"Josephine, are you all right?" Chester asked.

"Just a minute … I'm looking around."

The tiny room featured a small desk and chair. I pulled open the one and only desk drawer, stuffed with eight-by-ten black and white photos. I quickly flipped through the pile, noticing that they were of teenage girls and youngsters changing their clothes, tying the laces on their skates or just sitting on the benches that I remembered from the ladies' room upstairs. It looked to me like no one had actually posed for a picture.

I put the pictures back in the drawer, flipped off the light and returned to the tunnel. I took eight steps to the ladder, and looked back over my right shoulder at the wall safe. It was bigger than a car door. I imagined piles of money inside the safe. Gold bricks, actually.

"Josephine, someone's coming!" Chester hissed.

I hustled up the ladder and pulled the light string, then poked my head out and looked around like a gopher anticipating a herd of hungry cats. I heard Chester talking to someone.

"Yeah, lot's of improvements. Have you seen the new mural?" Chester said.

I watched Chester walk with a tall, older gentleman wearing a black suit across the rink to the south wall where my painters were working. I pulled myself out of the hole, quickly dropped the wooden square into place and joined my friends at the mural wall.

The gentleman turned out to be Mr. Bauer from the patent office next door. His place was sandwiched between the rink and the bingo parlor. He explained that he had just come from Mario's funeral. Said he wanted to make sure the man was dead.

My mouth dropped open.

"I know that sounds pretty harsh. You had to know him to understand," Bauer said as he ran fingers through thinning grey hair, then adjusted his hearing aid.

Chester excused himself and walked back to the building project.

"What was it that made Mr. Portello so unlikable?" I asked.

Mr. Bauer thought for a moment. "It's hard to say. He had a real sour personality, and he had a creepy way of looking at the young girl skaters. For me it was raising my rent."

"Are you saying that he owned the office you work in?"

"Yes, Mario owned the whole block, end-to-end until he sold the rink. But he couldn't stay away. He sold it to Ralph on the condition that he would always have a job here—the penny-pinching son of a gun. I never heard Ralph complain, maybe because he needed help running the rink."

Off-handedly, Mr. Bauer said something generically nice about the mural and left.

Alicia asked where I had been. I told her part of the truth, that I had been talking to Chester. I wasn't ready to tell her I had been down the rabbit hole discovering an underground room and some old photographs. She would want to know why I was down there and I didn't have a good answer. Why does a mountain climber climb a mountain? Because it's there.

I scratched out a few more Hokey Pokey notes and then helped paint them black. Black for death, the death of a man no one liked. I found myself almost liking Mario because of his under-dog status.

"Jo, you're acting like you're in outer space today. I don't think your heart is in this mural."

"You're right, Allie. It's not much of a challenge." If the mural had been more difficult or complicated, maybe my mind would have stayed with the program instead of drifting off to the "murder zone" and all the people who hated Mr. Portello. Despite my best intentions, my mind had already started to float away from the mural when Kyle startled me. His face looked flushed and worried.

"Josephine, like, ah … I have something—an errand to do this afternoon…."

"It's Ok, Kyle. We're ahead of schedule. Don't worry about taking the afternoon off."

"Thanks. I'll be here tomorrow." He dropped his

brush in water, picked up his helmet and stretched one long leg after the other out the back door.

"What's up with Kyle?" Alicia asked.

"I don't know. Maybe an errand, maybe a girl," I laughed. "Maybe we should take the afternoon off too. I want to pay a visit to Mario's widow. If she's like everyone else, her grieving ended before it started. You already know her, so you could go for a visit and bring me along."

"Jo, it was a big party with lots of people. She knows Ernie, but I doubt she would remember me."

"People always remember you, Allie. Anyway, I just want to help the woman. When I find the murderer, it will be a big relief for her to know who it was."

"Maybe she's like everyone else and thinks it was an accident," Alicia said. "Don't forget, Jo, today was Mario's funeral. Maybe she won't feel like talking to us."

After we hauled all the painting equipment to my truck, I talked Alicia into calling Ernie for Mrs. Portello's address. We were told she lived at 303 Martin Avenue, off of East Cliff Drive. If the house were close to the ocean, it would be expensive real estate.

Alicia called to arrange a visit.

High fog and coastal breezes are never conducive to good picnicking, so we ate our brown-bag lunches sitting in the cab of the pickup. Apparently, Santa Cruz's typical June-gloom had already started in May. I fired up the truck, and we followed the fog out to East Cliff Drive where a flat grey ocean gently licked at a string of vacant sandy beaches.

The Portello house was not hard to find. It was a large, two-story house at the corner of Martin and East Cliff Drive with an unobstructed view of the Pacific Ocean. Alicia and I climbed out of the truck, faced the ocean and sucked in some cool air. Hawkish gulls cut circles in the sky, eyeing us in case we had food to share.

"You go first, Allie," I said, waiting for her to walk to the front door.

"I told you I only met Gianna once...."

The door opened.

We hurried up a wide stone walkway and stepped up three steps to the door where a plump little lady wearing a black pant suit and matching flip flops greeted us as if we were old friends. She looked a decade younger than her deceased husband. Gianna's skin was smooth and brown like Alicia's. She had dark circles under her brown eyes with crow's feet at the outer corners. Her stylish grey-rooted black hair turned under in a perfect pageboy.

Alicia introduced us.

"Please sit down, ladies," Gianna said, as she plopped into a sofa opposite the one we sat on, which faced a giant rock fireplace. Displayed across the mantel were a dozen or more sympathy cards.

I fumbled for the right words until Alicia came up with the perfect sentiment, as she often did. She offered our condolences to Gianna, who smiled and told us she was doing well, all things considered.

"Gianna, do you know how your husband died?" I asked.

Alicia jammed her elbow in my side while the widow stared out the window.

"Of course I do. He was accidentally run over by a senior citizen," she said, as her eyes concentrated on the window behind us.

"I was the only witness to the crime...."

"What crime?" She leaned forward letting her eyes bore into mine.

"I hate to tell you this, but someone with excellent

driving skills crashed through the outer wall, flattened the office, put the car in reverse and quickly backed out the same hole, and hasn't been seen since. Know any seniors who could do that?"

"My word, Joan, I'm shocked. What are the police doing about it?"

"It's Josephine … and the police don't believe the act was intentional."

"Well, it sounds a little far-fetched to me. Did you happen to see who was driving?" Her black-penciled eyebrows pushed toward each other as she focused her attention on one perfectly polished fingernail.

"I'm here to talk to you because I saw what I saw. It's just too bad I couldn't see the driver. There was junk all over the windshield. I really need to know if someone wanted to kill your husband or did they want to destroy the rink, and Mario just happened to be there. You see, Alicia and I are painting a mural at the rink, and I'd really like to know if someone is going to come back and do more harm to the building—or us. No telling what a person that crazy will do." I took a deep breath.

My little speech brought Alicia into my corner. She asked Gianna if she had children. Were there any disgruntled family members, neighbors, business associates who would want to kill her husband?

Gianna just shook her pageboy.

"Gianna, can I use your bathroom?" I asked.

"Of course, dear, it's down the hall and the first right." She waved a hand at it.

I heard Alicia and Gianna discussing Ernie's work at the university, as I poked my head into a few rooms and made a detour through the kitchen. I opened the kitchen door and peeked into the garage. She had a shiny black Lexus parked there, obviously in new condition. If they had a second car, it was missing.

I closed the door and stepped back onto a squishy something that screeched like a cat on fire. The black cat pulled himself loose. It shook its paw and ran straight to the living room.

I followed.

Gianna and Alicia gave me strange looks.

"Sorry. I don't know how your cat got his foot under mine," I shrugged. "Allie, we need to go … remember the, ah, meeting?" I checked my watch for effect.

Alicia obediently stood up and followed me to the door.

Gianna gave her a hug as I stepped outside.

Once we were settled into our seats and traveling along the city streets, Alicia giggled, and asked why Gianna's cat was so upset. I ignored the cat subject and went straight to the black car in the garage, the separate bedrooms for Mario and Gianna and the fact that I hadn't seen one single photo of the dear departed husband anywhere in the house.

"That doesn't mean anything, Jo. Lots of people have black cars and sleep in separate bedrooms. Maybe they didn't own a camera...."

"Oh, he owned one all right." Alicia brought up the subject so I jumped in and told her about the trap door, tunnel and drawer full of old photos of girls dressing. The pictures were pretty tame by modern standards, but obviously taken without the girls' knowledge or permission.

Alicia said she was shocked by Mario's actions … and mine. She and David never understood my need for justice. Even Mom rarely understood the forces that drove me. They believed law enforcement officials would take care of any and all law-breakers. So where was the police involvement in Mario's death? I met Sergeant Fishburn. He was convinced the whole thing was an accident. What about hit-and-run for starters?

I dropped Alicia at her car and drove home. It was mid-afternoon and I hadn't thought about the kitten all day. I opened the front door.

From out of nowhere, the yellow bomber leaped onto my shoulder, and slid down my back. I heard something rip.

Solow hung his head in shame as I took an inventory of broken household items.

CHAPTER EIGHT

I woke up Thursday morning with "fifty ways to get rid of the bratty cat" on my mind. I rolled over, setting off a screech-leap-run demonstration.

"Sorry, Bratworse, I didn't know you were there."

He bounced across the room, crawled in bed with Solow, and looked back at me with blinky eyes.

I rolled out of bed wondering if I had been sleeping with the kitten all night. My feelings of guilt quickly faded as Bratworse and Solow happily followed me down the hall to the back door. I let them out, and watched them through the kitchen window.

Solow shadowed Bratworse everywhere until Fluffy showed up across the field on a fence post, twitching her tail—her way of saying, "Catch me if you can." Solow blasted across the patio at basset speed and bounced through half an acre of spring grasses, ears flying like whirligigs.

I headed for the shower, knowing full well how the Fluffy chase would end. Fluffy was a well-behaved cat except when it came to torturing Solow. At least Bratworse would never be unkind to his protector—but still, I needed to spend some quality time with the kitten, teaching him a few manners. I realized it wasn't the kitty's fault he was still a baby and didn't know the rules of the house.

After a quick breakfast, I set out the kitten's milk, arranged his bed and tried not to think about the damage he would probably do to my house while I was gone.

I drove along San Juan Road at a pretty good clip

until I came up behind half-a-dozen cars all crawling along at ten miles an hour. Up ahead, I saw the cause— a giant tractor on treads sending out clods of dirt and clouds of dust as it inched along the pavement. When the on-coming lane was finally clear of traffic, all the cars passed the tractor, one-by-one.

Still driving north, my usual forty-minute drive turned into an hour and a half when traffic came to a halt on Highway One near Capitola. Between the roadwork and the gawkers, I figured half the county would be late to work. But my friends weren't late. Even Ralph's car was parked in the lot when I arrived. I parked next to Alicia's Volvo and carried my toolbox full of squeeze bottles of paint into the building.

Alicia and Kyle saw me, trotted out to the truck and hauled in the rest of our supplies while I looked for Ralph. I found him in the center of the framed office, on his knees, watching Chester navigate the skinny little underground ladder.

My cheeks blushed. I had forgotten to lock the trap door.

Ralph looked up. "Josephine, this is amazing. They tell me you found this trap door."

"Yeah, I noticed the square cut in the floor...."

Ralph turned his attention back to Chester. "Did you find any more rooms down there?"

"Just the little office. I'm coming up." Chester squeezed his shoulders together and inched his way out of the hole. He dropped a hand full of photos on the floor, and Ralph picked them up.

"These pictures look old ... maybe thirty or forty years? What do you think, Josephine?" I don't know why he asked me since he was two years my senior.

"Judging by the clothing styles, I would say they are about forty years old." I would have been ten at the time.

"Whoa, this girl is undressing ... and this one's smoking...." Ralph's jaw dropped. "Who took these pictures anyway?"

"It had to be Mario. He was small enough to fit down the rabbit hole and this was his place for almost fifty years," I said. "He's the one who had the underground room built."

"How do you know that, Josephine? When I bought the building he didn't tell me about the tunnel and room."

"Mr. Trippy told me."

"Very trippy," Chester laughed, brushing dust and cobwebs off the seat of his pants. Like a couple of ten-year-old boys, the two men carefully examined the pictures.

A blank piece of yellowed notepaper had fallen to the floor. I picked it up and held it to the light, noticing impressions made by a pen or pencil. I folded the paper and stuffed it in my pocket, making a mental note to examine it later. I heard snickering.

"Hey, Josephine, look at this one." Chester waved a picture at me.

"Oh my ... she's a hairy beast," I said, and then wished I hadn't said it. I thought about how it would feel to look like King Kong while attending junior high school. The poor girl was big for her age and had dark body hair covering her arms and legs. Her face looked familiar in a way.

It was time to leave the "stuck in junior high" man-boys. Seeing glimpses of girl's underwear as entertainment struck me as pathetically infantile.

My friends and I finished painting the last of the music notes before lunchtime. After lunch, I began chalking in the lyrics to the Hokey Pokey song. As I drew and my friends painted, I thought about what a sad, twisted little man Mario must have been. Did his wife know about his strange behavior?

"Jo to earth, Jo to earth," Alicia laughed. When she finally got my attention she said, "Do you want the letters like this or thicker?"

"Thicker by half an inch," I said, wondering if Mario had ever physically hurt anyone. The old black and white pictures were rather artistic. I didn't get the feeling they were suggestive. They were more like snapshots of girls doing what girls do, including their smiles and tears. Before I judged the old man too harshly, I wanted to see the contents of the safe ... but what if some really bad pictures were hidden in there? Until someone found the combination, I could only speculate.

"Josephine, you missed a letter," Kyle said.

"Oops, I'll erase this part and try again. Thanks, Kyle." I double-checked the sheet music, focused my distracted grey matter and managed to finish the lettering by four o'clock. My painters and I were the last to leave the building.

As soon as Alicia and Kyle drove away, I unlocked the back door, reentered the building and headed for the underground room. I turned all the lights on and hunted for a combination to the safe. All I found were a few yellowed scraps of paper tacked to a piece of corkboard on the wall opposite the safe; a list of chemicals, the first verse of Hokey Pokey and a phone number. I stuffed the three notes into my pocket and moved on to the little room.

I heard muffled footsteps overhead. As I poked my head out of the trap door, my eyes glommed onto a pair of purple ankle boots with pink laces. Then came the black net tights, pink shorts and black knit tank top with matching visor. Above the visor, blond chia hair sprouted upward like dry grass.

"Ah, Bonnie, how did you get in here?" I croaked,

wearing a ripe tomato complexion.

"Someone left the back door unlocked," she smirked.

I crawled out of the hole and stood up—up to Bonnie's chin. I figured we were close in age but she was six inches taller and many pounds heavier. She had wide shoulders and muscles everywhere.

I finally pulled myself together. After all, I belonged there. She didn't. Ralph hired me to paint a mural. Why should I feel intimidated? What was she doing in the building anyway?

"I was just leaving, Bonnie. I'll walk you out," I said.

"After you tell me what you're doing down there," she smiled, as I covered the hole.

"I accidentally discovered this door to an underground room … Ralph knows about it. I told him. Chester and Alicia know about it too," I babbled. "I've been trying to figure out why someone would want to kill Mr. Portello, and I thought there might be clues down there."

"Really … how interesting. Find anything down there?"

"Just some old photographs."

Bonnie adjusted her smile.

"I'm going home now. I'll walk you to the door."

We made it to the parking lot without any more discussion about the underground area. Bonnie headed down to her Bingo gig, and I drove to the market in Watsonville.

Robert looked up from his check stand and gave me a nod as I pushed my shopping basket through heavy cart traffic to the produce aisle. I pitied a mom with two munchkins sitting in her cart and a third baby strapped to her chest as she fingered avocados to find a ripe one. Wet diaper smell sent me hustling to the next aisle for canned cat food.

Robert walked up to me. "You're buying cat food?"

"I inherited a kitten...."

"Ah, that's nice...."

"Not really. It bites, scratches and destroys everything in its path."

"How big is this kitten?"

"Bratworse fits in one hand. I think he's feral, or at least hyperactive and a bit crazy. I'm hoping he'll outgrow it."

"With a name like Bratworse, he'll be scarred for life. Give him a nice name like Fluffy or Tiger, and he'll be a well-adjusted cat when he grows up," Robert said, sounding like a PhD with a house full of well-adjusted kidlettes.

I rolled my eyes and thought about the devil-cat named Fluffy who had tortured Solow since he was a puppy.

"If this cat doesn't straighten up, I'll send him to therapy at your house." I rolled my cart to a checkout and Robert rang up my groceries.

"Anything new on the roller rink rubout?" he asked.

"I'm trying to find someone who hated Mario enough to do such a thing. Trouble is, Mario had no friends and everyone who knew him disliked him, but not enough to murder him. See you later, Robert." I hauled my bags of groceries to the truck, loaded them into the back and pulled the top down. Twenty minutes later, I parked in front of my house.

David's Miata pulled up beside my truck. He helped bring in the groceries.

I looked around, expecting a surprise hit from the brat. Nothing happened and the house looked the same as I had left it.

"David, where are the kids ... I mean Solow and Bratworse?"

"On my patio. I checked on them this morning and found your little trapeze artist stuck in the bottom of the blue glass vase on the side table. I fished him out and took him home. Of course, Solow came too. They've been romping around my back yard all day. No problem."

I felt like a failure, an uncaring mother, a total witch.

"Bratworse didn't run away?" I asked.

"Heck no! He likes it here. Three squares and Solow to keep him warm. I think this is the best life he's ever known." David helped put the groceries away and then walked me down to his back yard. Solow and the kitten were stretched out, soaking up the last of Thursday's sunshine.

I picked up the little kitten and held him to my cheek. He was half asleep and completely calm for a change. Now if he would only stay that way. I held him with one hand and gave Solow an ear rub with the other. And then my attention went to David.

Darling David had prepared a lovely dinner for two and an evening of movies and relaxation. Even the best-laid plans can be improved upon—so we did. And it was a night to remember.

CHAPTER NINE

I woke up early Friday morning still living in a dream. I had dreamt about David and our two sets of twins. I sat up and shook my head, trying to shake away images of bawling twin kittens and a set of howling bassets, all wearing bonnets, and stuffed into a baby carriage. I tried to hold onto my favorite parts of the dream, like the quality time with David.

Our Thursday night dinner date had been fun and romantic until the Mario subject came up, and David realized how involved I was in the murder case. For the sake of peace between us, I cleverly changed the subject to romance.

Solow and Bratworse woke up and begged to go outside. I let the little beggars out, and then headed for my best friend, Mr. Coffee who always brewed a decent cup of java without any backtalk. I showered and dressed while I waited for my cup of Joe.

I poured steaming coffee into my favorite mug, and poked my head in the refrigerator, looking for a tasty breakfast idea. The phone rang, jarring me out of my rummaging.

"Josephine, this is Ashley Rattini. I, ah … was talking to Chester recently and he said you've been snooping, that is, you have experience solving criminal cases like murder. I wanted to tell you about someone who might have wanted to hurt Mr. Portello. Are you there … Josephine?"

My heart skipped a beat. "Yes, I'm listening. Who is the person?"

"I thought we could go to lunch and discuss it, that

is, if you have time today."

"That sounds great, Ashley. Noonish?"

"Sure, I'll meet you at the rink." She hung up.

I put a bowl of water outside for Solow and Bratworse, placed a little bowl of cat food on the patio table and a big helping of Solow's favorite kibble under the table. I planned to leave the animals outside since Solow had never ever wandered away from home. I figured the kitten would stay with him and my house would not be shredded when I got home. Besides, it had worked well for David.

I arrived at the rink and went straight to work on the pepper tree, feeling good about not having a monster loose in my house, and looking forward to hearing what Ashley wanted to tell me. I hoped her information would break the case so that David would stop being upset with me. I had already told Alicia and Kyle about my lunch plans so they made plans of their own.

Ashley arrived at twelve sharp looking ten years younger than Ralph, except for her crow's feet and smile lines. Ashley and I walked two blocks to Charlie Hong Kong's, a popular noodle place. We ordered our food at the little window and found a place to sit. The food arrived and a minute later, my friends walked in.

Alicia nudged Kyle and took him to a table at the opposite end of the room.

Ashley fussed with a strand of strawberry blond hair as we made small talk. I wondered how she managed to keep her weight down and look so young. She wore itsy bitsy designer stretch jeans from G's Boutique around the corner, where they catered to twenties–thirties gals. I recognized her sequin top from the same mannequin in the window wearing the jeweled jeans. I wished I could fit into such things, but my mature body looked better in more conservative styles.

"So, Ashley, what information do you have about

the murder?"

She flinched. I think the "murder" word startled her. "Well, maybe it was murder," she said softly. I barely heard her over the crowd of lunchers. She closed her eyes for a moment, opened them and told me about another shop owner who rented from Mr. Portello. His name was Grady Hammer, an African American barber who also cut and styled women's hair.

"Why do you think Grady's the one?"

She leaned closer. "They say he has a temper, and he was furious when Mario said he was going to raise the rent."

"There's a lot of that raising the rent going around. Any other reason?" I asked.

"No, isn't that enough?" She squirmed in her seat.

"Well, it's worth looking into. How many properties did Mario rent out?"

"Just three—Bonnie's Bingo, the patent office and the barbershop. He inherited the whole block of businesses from his father who died when Mario was in his twenties. Mario razed a grocery store half a century ago and built the roller rink in its place."

"That was a nice thing to do for the community; so why did he ask for more rent?"

"Bonnie thinks he was raising rents because he was planning to, like, sell everything, and the higher the rent, the more the places would seem to be worth to a potential buyer, supposedly." Ashley twirled noodles on her chopsticks. A clump of hair fell into her eyelashes. She flipped it back, nervously repeating the flip every two minutes.

I hardly tasted my noodle dish because my thoughts kept darting back to the line-up of suspects. Three renters had been angry with Mario. Even his own sister and wife didn't like him very much. But so far, I hadn't found anyone with a solid reason to murder him.

After lunch, Ashley said she wanted to walk up the street and pick up a few items at Just G's Boutique.

I thanked her for confiding in me and walked in the other direction with Alicia and Kyle, back to the rink. As we passed the barbershop, I stopped for a moment to look through the window. The little shop had one barber's chair. I recognized Ralph as the victim sitting in the big swivel chair with half his wavy black hair on the floor, the other half barely covering the top of his squarish head. He and Hammer were talking—until they saw me.

Grady glanced in my direction. I wondered if he cut his own hair. It wouldn't be hard to do, just run the shaver over his head every couple days.

Feeling red-faced, I smiled at the two men and quickly caught up to my friends.

"Aren't you the big flirt?" Alicia teased, as we entered the rink and went back to work.

I went through the motions of drawing and painting, but my mind kept bouncing back to the murder puzzle. Was Grady angry enough to kill?

Carrying a large bag of something from G's, Ashley entered the rink an hour later. If the two-carat studs in her ears and the big diamond on a gold chain around her neck were real, she was already wearing a fortune. Ralph must have done well at something before buying the rink.

Ashley marched through the building, heading for the back door and parking lot. Halfway across the rink, she stopped for a moment to watch us paint.

"It's coming along nicely, isn't it?" she said, and continued her journey, not waiting for an answer.

I remembered something and ran out to her car as she was getting in. The car rims glinted in the afternoon sun.

"Ashley, where does Mr. Hammer live?"

"In the two little rooms behind the barbershop."

"Thanks ... and thanks for lunch. If you think of any other suspects, let me know."

She nodded, waved and drove past my pickup and out to the street.

My Mazda pickup made me smile. We had been through so much together. I told myself I would never trade my truck for a fancy new BMW. Those rims were too shiny for my taste. I scanned the parking lot and spotted Bonnie leaning against the back wall of her bingo parlor having a smoke. I decided to walk over and have a chat with the woman.

"Bonnie, what's up?"

She took a long drag and blew a donut hole in the air. "Nothing new here." She let out a crusty laugh.

"Do you know the barber up the street? I'm thinking of getting a haircut."

"You mean Grady. He's pretty good with hair." She absently touched a spike of yellow straw bursting up and over her lavender visor.

I instantly decided I would never let the man touch my hair. "Is he a friend of yours?"

"I'm a customer. I guess you could say we're friends. What's it to you?"

"It's just that everyone's upset about the rent hike...."

"Yeah, yeah, the lease, taxes and crime. Can't we all just get along?" Bonnie snorted, as she stood up and turned to go inside.

"Wait, what's this about a lease?"

"Mario wanted each of us to sign a six-month lease."

"What's so bad about that?"

"We've always paid our rent month-to-month. We liked it that way. Besides that, the monthly rate was going to go up and we would have to pay for all the utilities."

Before I could react, she stepped inside and closed the door.

I opened the door and followed Bonnie through a crowded storage area, ending in a spacious room full of tables, chairs, country music and bright lights. My image of quiet rickety old people playing bingo instantly evaporated. The tables were covered with brightly colored tablecloths, and a series of framed posters and photographs lined the walls. Groups of seniors sat at various card tables playing games such as chess, dominoes and five-card-stud.

I noticed a spirited poker game in progress between four elderly ladies sitting around a table in the far corner. One lady, wearing her black wig half-cocked, made eye contact.

"Josephine, my dear, come here," Myrtle waved.

I made my way over to the poker game where Mom and Dad's neighbor pushed her chair back, stood up and gave me a hug, sending her wig a little more to the right.

"Myrtle, what are you ... I mean, I didn't know you liked to play poker."

"There's a lot you don't know about me, dear," she chuckled. The other three ladies giggled, as if Myrtle had outrageous secrets she never shared. I knew better. Mom knew everything about her friend and neighbor for the last forty years, and all of it was as dry as forty-year-old wallpaper.

Bonnie finally saw me and began showing me around. She seemed to be very proud of the business she had built up, pointing out various games and naming people as we moved from table to table. One table had a giant half-finished puzzle laid out with three elderly men completely focused on finding the right puzzle pieces. A pair of beautiful long legs and high-heeled shoes began to take shape.

"Bonnie, how do you, ah, make money? Like, what do you charge...."?

"I charge each person two dollars an hour for use of the table, and a dollar for a cup of coffee or tea. It pays the rent and a little bit for me to live on."

"How much did your rent go up?"

"Let's just say, the new lease would have been impossible for me to pay. Thankfully, Mario's wife doesn't know about the lease idea. She collected the rents Monday and didn't say a word about changing anything." Bonnie poured herself a cup of coffee. "Would you like a cup?"

"Thanks, but I need to get back to work." I had almost forgotten the mural and my hardworking painters. "By the way, is that you in the roller derby picture?" I pointed to a framed twelve by eighteen-inch color action shot where someone with hairy arms topped a three-player pile-up.

"Yeah, that's me. I knocked the you-know-what out of those sissy girls. The refs weren't too happy. Actually, I was ejected. I refused to go, so three refs dragged me outside," she laughed. "Best game ever!"

"OK, I better get back to work. See yah." I felt sorry for anyone who tangled with Bonnie.

As I drove through Santa Cruz, I made a last-second decision and zipped right past the entrance to the freeway. I headed across town toward the coast and Gianna's place. Her neighborhood looked peaceful. My tires scraped the curb and came to a stop.

I stepped down to the pavement, marveling at the sound of giant waves crashing along the beach half a block away. The fresh smell of rotting seaweed and briny water instantly took me back to age fourteen. Body surfing with my cousin had been a blast until the undertow got hold of me. I didn't fight it, just held my breath for ages, and when the powerful ocean finally let go, I popped up gasping.

My instincts told me someone was behind me. I turned to see two women walking at a brisk pace up the sidewalk toward my truck. It was Gianna and a tall, slim, fiftyish-looking woman with stringy brown hair pulled into a ponytail. They fast-walked right by me. Gianna was blowing air, working hard to keep up with Ms. Long Legs.

"Gianna, yoou whoo, Mrs. Portello!"

The women stopped and looked back, breathing hard.

"I'm sorry, Joan. I didn't see you there." Gianna said.

"It's Josephine, Alicia's friend," I said, punctuating my words with a smile.

"Josephine, this is my friend and neighbor, Nicki."

Nicki looked at my paint clothes like I was an escapee from the zoo.

Gianna didn't seem to notice. "What are you doing in this neighborhood, my dear?"

"I found out some interesting things I'd like to share with you," I said, feeling like a troll next to the sophisticated widow and her athletic-looking friend. Gianna was the kind of person who looked dressed up even when she dressed down, plus she held the title, "Professor," at the University.

"In that case, let's go inside. See you later, Nicki."

Nicki pounded her Nikes past Gianna's front lawn and disappeared around the corner.

We entered the house. Gianna led me to an over-stuffed chair positioned directly under a large ornately framed portrait of a young woman, possibly Gianna a few decades ago. Her looks had not faded, just matured. As Alicia would say, "Sixty-five is the new fifty."

I told her about the hole in the floor at the rink and what we found in the little room below, hoping for a reaction. I watched her expressionless face, wondering if she already knew about Mario's strange hobby. I decided Gianna would make a great poker player, or maybe she didn't give a hoot about anything the old man did. She raised an eyebrow when I mentioned the photographs of young girls, but it relaxed when I said the pictures were not particularly risqué or offensive.

The one thing I did not talk about was Mario's idea to turn rent money into lease money. If Gianna didn't know anything about it, who was I to spoil it for Bonnie, Mr. Bauer and the barber? I left the house feeling like I had unloaded a lot on Gianna, but she had left me with nothing new ... again.

Driving home, I decided to stop at Dings and Dents on Freedom Boulevard. I took the Green Valley exit into Watsonville, made a right at Freedom and parked in front of the body shop. I asked the girl at the desk a few questions like, "Did you guys work on a badly dented black sedan recently?"

"We cannot give out that type of information," the girl repeated after every question.

I felt like pounding my head on the counter. Probably all the body shops had the same policy of "mum's the word." I decided I would have to look elsewhere for the killer's car, thanked the young woman and left. It was time to head home and forget about the rink. And then I remembered the kittywampus zoo I was going home to.

CHAPTER TEN

Ah, the luxury of sleeping late on a Saturday morning. That was my plan until a certain kitten became airborne and landed on my face with a banshee scream.

Half asleep, I instinctively swiped at the cat knocking it to the floor.

Solow berated me with a couple sharp barks. But all was quickly forgotten as I crawled out of bed and led my four-legged dependants down the hall to the back door. After a good romp, they wanted in. I poured kibble, scooped kitty goop from a can and made myself a cup of coffee and an omelet.

I sat at the kitchen table enjoying my lovely egg dish. Suddenly, Bratworse leaped into my lap, but fell back, hooking his claws into my robe. As he dangled helplessly, I pried his tiny nails away from the fabric and gently set him on the kitchen floor. I turned back to finish my omelet, but a second later Bratworse was caught in my robe again. I peeled him off, opened the back door and dropped him outside. His long-eared nursemaid followed.

Once the boys were out of my hair, I finished breakfast, showered and dressed for a day of nothing in particular.

The phone rang.

Alicia asked if I had plans for the evening. One of her Santa Cruz friends had given her tickets to the Roller Derby. Even though the rink was not completely restored yet, Ralph would host the event. I said I would pick her up at seven.

If David had plans for us, they would have to be afternoon plans. As it turned out, he took me to lunch at one of my favorite restaurants, the Haute Enchilada in Moss Landing, where the artsy ambiance was as stimulating as the food.

As we sat on the Haute patio sipping iced tea, I told David about Alicia's tickets to the roller derby and my curiosity about the game. I told him about Bonnie and how she had raised my interest in the sport, and then, coincidentally, I finally had a chance to see the skating Sirens first hand. It was hard for me to resist David's idea of a perfect evening, but there would be other magical nights.

At first, going to the Women's Flat Track Roller Derby felt like going to work, same neighborhood, same building, but instead of nine in the morning it was early evening. Ralph stood at the front door taking tickets and Ashley sold popcorn and ice cream at the counter inside.

I followed Alicia to the fifth row out of five, of bone-breaker wooden benches where we found a bench with room for one more person. Both of us squished into the little space while people on either side inched closer to each other, sucking in their muffin tops.

Competing with an announcer and the speaker system, Alicia tried to explain the rules of the game to me. She said each team used five players at a time, one jammer and four blockers. The jammer wore a cap with a star on the side over her regular helmet. They scored points only when they were able to blast their way through the other team's blockers who literally set up a roadblock, a chain of blockers across the track. Anyone knocked out of bounds had to circle back and try again.

"Allie, what's the point of the game? I don't see goal posts or anything."

"Like I told you, every time a jammer makes it

around the circle, the team earns points. The blockers try to stop the jammers...."

"If you say so...." I said, scrutinizing the oval track.

Someone blew a whistle. Everyone stood up for the National Anthem and then settled down in their seats, or, in the case of dozens of people behind us, stood for the next two hours.

The Silicon Valley Roller Girls filed onto the oval flat track looking like polished clones in their white helmets, green and white tank tops and shorts with black knee and wrist pads. They completed several laps, impressing the crowd with synchronized exercises to help them limber up.

Then came the Santa Cruz team, the Seabright Sirens in basic blue and black, accented with colorful leggings and tattoos, not to mention a head of blue hair, a pink one and a gold one. They exercised around the rink showing off their expert moves and decorative attire with their roller derby names printed on the backs of their regulation tank tops. Names like *Baby Girl, Merry Pain, Toxic Moxie, Rotten Weiler, Unleashed, Kamikaze Rozy, Checkout, Rocker and Patti Smithereens.*

A whistle blew.

Eight helmeted gals positioned themselves into two four-person blockades while two jammers waited on the sideline for a signal. One of the six referees blasted his whistle and the two jammers charged the human blockades.

Spectators screamed until I thought my ears would burst.

Even my demure friend, Alicia, stood up, waved her arms and shouted.

Toxic Moxie, wearing black and blue, danced side-to-side behind three women in white and suddenly turned her slender body sideways, slipping right through the blockade. She leaned forward and fast-skated around the rink only to tackle the blockade again. Four times in a row, she managed to outsmart the Silicon Valley gals.

I watched the Santa Cruz team rack up three times as many points as the Valley team. The room became hot and stuffy and the noise was unbearable. I looked around for Bonnie, and decided she was probably past roller-derby age and busy at the bingo parlor.

After an hour of shoving and tripping and the crowd yelling at the top of their lungs, I was wishing for a glass of cold water. Perspiration trickled down my spine. At halftime, the two teams took a break. I headed for the refreshment stand, bought two ice cream bars and delivered one of them to Alicia. We ate the bars outside on the lawn with fifty or more fans.

When we heard a whistle, we followed the crowd back inside. Within minutes, my head was pounding again. The roar of the skates echoed from ear-to-ear and the ice cream had given me brain-freeze. I grabbed my purse and shouted to Alicia I had a headache and was going to step outside for a minute.

Outside, the evening air felt wonderful, fresh and cool. I shivered and decided to walk to the back of the building to get my sweater out of the truck. Streetlights lit the way to the parking lot. As I rounded the back corner of the building, light and music flowed from Bonnie's back door. Ten yards further there was the roar of the rink from an open window.

As I marched on, searching out my pickup in the eerie yellow lamplight, a movement at the far end of the parking lot caught my attention, not close enough to be a threat, but I was curious. A man I recognized as Grady the barber carried a briefcase and rolled a suitcase across the parking lot to his black car. I watched as he opened the trunk and stuffed everything inside, and then climbed into the driver's seat.

My heart pounded as I watched the potential killer prepare to leave town. Did he suspect I was on to him? I hurried over to my pickup, climbed in and turned the key.

Grady cruised through the parking lot sporting one red tail-light and one broken white one, probably resulting from his car smashing through walls where poor old Mario worked. Maybe he had the front end repaired and forgot about the taillight. He turned right onto Seabright and stopped at the Soquel Avenue intersection.

I cautiously pulled my truck up to a white Ford pickup that had cut in front of me.

Grady and the white truck turned right. I followed, but not too closely. I had already forgotten about my headache. I knew what I had to do. I would simply follow the barber until he arrived at his destination, and then I would turn him in to the police.

I stuck my hand in my purse and felt for my phone, just to make sure it was there if I needed it. It rang as I touched it. My hand jerked back. I decided to concentrate on driving and call whomever it was later. My eyes were glued to Grady's left rear tail-light, which stood out from all the red ones on the road. The white pickup turned right just before Grady took the Highway One on-ramp, but two cars squeezed in between my suspect and me.

I spotted Grady in the fast lane and sped up, passing a few cars and an eighteen-wheeler lit up like a Christmas tree with red, gold and green lights outlining the long trailer and more lights up front. Right after the Emeline exit, Grady swerved into the right lane and exited to Highway 17 with me stuck to his rear like a pair of polyester pants straight out of the dryer.

Highway 17 isn't for sissies. It has four lanes of

torturous turns that curl up and around and down various mountains at break-your-neck speeds. The only thing more dangerous would be the Roller Derby. Oh my gosh! I had forgotten all about Alicia. I couldn't go back. The next exit was thirty miles away. I hoped Alicia would find a ride home—and forgive me.

Grady stayed in the fast lane at just a titch over the speed limit. I closed in on his bumper, hoping he would speed up and attract the attention of a highway patrolman. Where were they when I needed one? Not an officer anywhere. Unfortunately, my truck was no match for Grady's car on the up-hill climbs. Each time the highway leveled off a bit, I caught up, just in time to fall behind on the next incline.

Finally, we passed the summit and headed downhill into Santa Clara County. My truck was excellent on the downhill grade as I shadowed the white tail-light past Los Gatos and Campbell, into San Jose. The tail-light switched lanes. I followed. Someone honked. I ignored it. We exited onto Highway 280 North. The honker rode my tail until he finally got his anger under control somewhere around Los Altos.

Traffic was heavy for ten o'clock at night.

Grady signaled and moved to the right across three lanes of traffic.

I followed, thinking, "What am I doing here and why are there so many people traveling this highway at night?" But I had too much invested in Grady's capture and kept going.

Grady took the exit into Redwood City and I followed. Two cars merged into the spot between my truck and Grady's car. I honked and then felt ashamed, remembering the enraged honker who had tailgated me for so many miles. I strained to see the white tail-light as it turned left at an intersection and pulled into a well-lit gas station.

While Grady pumped gas, I pumped forty dollars worth of fuel into my tank. I gave him a head start out of the station but caught up just before the on-ramp to Highway 280, where a row of street lights ended.

Less than an hour later, the highway dumped us onto the Bay Bridge. My heart pounded. What was I doing in San Francisco, heading to Oakland? My original plan seemed a little crazy, but it was too late to go back. At ten-thirty, traffic was still heavy. The roller derby would have ended—I wondered how Alicia would get home. Would she ever speak to me again?

I followed Grady off the bridge, through Oakland neighborhoods and into Berkeley with its tree-lined streets, bicycles and late-night pedestrians. I knew a little bit about the college town because my two sets of grandparents had lived in Oakland within a mile of Berkeley most of their lives. A wave of sadness washed over me. I was only minutes away from their homes, but couldn't drop in for a visit with the "Grands" because they had all passed away. I missed them for the millionth time.

Reminiscing cost me. I almost lost sight of the white tail-light. Adrenalin pumped, I sped up, whipped around a corner and slammed on the brakes just inches behind Grady's bumper. The light turned green and off we went, over the railroad tracks, up Broadway and down the other side. It was a constant game of trying not to lose sight of the tail-light without getting too close.

My phone rang again. No time for talking, so I let it ring.

Grady led me off the main boulevard into a small hamlet that looked closed up for the night, except for one gas station and a medical facility. At first, I thought the building looked like a church. After a closer look from the curb, I decided it was a church converted into a convalescent hospital. My truck idled as Grady hurried inside. After a few minutes, I decided he wasn't coming out right away and shut down the engine.

After a few minutes of stewing, I marched into the repurposed building and talked to the attendant at the front desk.

"Hi, I, ah … I'm looking for Mr. Hammer …."

"That way, room sixteen." The nurse pointed.

I walked past room sixteen, turning my head to catch a glimpse of Grady and his grandmother. Ms. Hammer didn't look good, hooked up to all kinds of tubes, and her grandson looked devastated. Could a guy who loves his grandmother commit murder? Maybe I had been too quick to pass judgment on the fellow. I kept walking, making several right turns until I was back at the front desk.

"Can you tell me how Ms. Hammer is doing?" I asked the night nurse.

"She'll be around for a few more days. But with cancer, you never can tell for sure."

My eyes stung. What was I thinking? The poor man just wanted a little time with his dying grandmother. Suddenly I felt exhausted. I checked my watch. It was almost eleven-thirty. I sunk into a waiting room chair, my head nodded and my nightmare began.

I dreamt I came home from work to find that Solow, Fluffy and Bratworse had taken over my house. All the old furniture was gone, replaced with scratching posts, fire hydrants and Frisbees. I opened the refrigerator and found a dozen little brothers and sisters of Bratworse. They scampered into the dining room and began climbing the drapes.

In the dream, the phone was ringing, but I couldn't get past all the animals to answer it. David appeared and grabbed my shoulder. Finally my eyes opened and focused on the nurse standing beside my chair.

"Miss, I'm afraid you can't sleep here. It's against regulations."

"I didn't mean to fall asleep. I'll be going now...."

Before I had time to stand up, Grady walked up the hall and stopped in front of my chair.

"Don't I know you from Santa Cruz?" he asked.

"I don't think we met, but I saw you in your barbershop yesterday," I yawned.

"Oh, right. What are you doing up here?"

I hoped he didn't notice my face reddening.

"I had to look in on a friend," I said.

The nurse rolled her eyes to the ceiling and left us to our conversation. Did she think I was an old cougar chasing after a young stud muffin? The bigger question was, why in the world had I suspected this nice young man of murder?

"My name is Josephine Stuart. I'm painting a mural at the rink...."

"I'm Grady Hammer," he said, putting his hand out. We shook hands. Mine was wet as a swamp rat. He continued, "And I saw your work the other day when Chester let me in. That's really something about that secret room under the rink. I told Chester I might be able to help unlock the safe—that is, if Ralph needs help. Did a little work, ah, in that area a long time ago, before barber school. You look tired, Josephine. Can I get you a cup of coffee?"

"That would be wonderful, Grady."

He came back with two coffees and a couple of Danishes.

"Thank you. This coffee will help to get me home."

"Wow, all the way back to Santa Cruz tonight?"

"Further south than that, I'm afraid." I opened a packet of phony cream and emptied it into my coffee.

Grady took a sip of the hot vending machine brew.

"I'll be staying at my grandmother's house tonight—

maybe longer."

"How is your grandmother?" I asked.

"Old, tired and ready to go," he smiled weakly. "I'll miss her."

"I'm sorry...." We ate our pastries without another word, just a goodbye when it was time for me to leave.

Grady walked me to my truck and wished me well.

I climbed in and sat there, too choked up to say another word, and wishing I wasn't looking at over a hundred miles of road ahead of me. I watched the barber drive his car into the moonless night until his tail-light finally disappeared from view. I turned the key, punched up the heater and in no time, the cab was cozy-warm.

I called Alicia, and left an explanation-apology type message on her phone.

All that was left was a long drive home.

CHAPTER ELEVEN

Sunday morning happened without me. In my dreams, I heard David's voice, phones ringing, footsteps and a hound dog howling. But all the noises fit neatly into my dreams as I slept on and on till noon. At twelve, I finally rolled out of bed and dragged my stiff neck and sore back into the shower.

I shuddered in the warm water when I remembered how I had left my best friend at the rink without a ride home, and David without an explanation of any kind. But how does one explain an impulsive act to a person like David? Following Grady made perfect sense to me at the time, but my sweet boyfriend usually looked at things differently. He was cautious, methodical and logical.

I heard his voice coming from the kitchen as I wiped mist off the mirror, stared into a pair of puffy eyes and spent extra time on my hair and makeup. When all the blow-drying, tweezing and powdering was done, I padded back to my bedroom and pulled on a deep green shirt that matched my eyes and my best butt-minimizer jeans. A pair of cute flip-flops and some jewelry, and I was ready to face the new day.

I found David in the living room watching a game of golf on TV.

David pulled his eyes from the tube and smiled. "There's my Josie."

Solow greeted me with a pounding tail.

Bratworse jumped off David's lap and climbed up my jeans.

I held him and snuggled my face into his soft fur.

"Good morning, David. Ouch! You little devil...." I dropped Bratworse to the floor.

"It's not morning, sweetie," he grinned. "Are you OK? That must have been some roller derby you went to."

"Yeah, it was," I rubbed the back of my neck with my hand. "Thanks for taking care of the boys for me."

"No problem. What's for lunch?"

"I'll put something together." I was hungry, but needed a little time to gather my wits. I put Mr. Coffee to work and searched the fridge for an easy lunch. Nothing appealed to me. While my head was in the fridge, I tossed a few ugly specimens in the garbage and sponged off the shelves. A thorough cleaning would have to wait.

David entered the kitchen asking if he could help.

"I have an idea," I said. "I'll take us to the Grill for lunch, but you can drive."

David grumbled something and I cut him off. "You're so old fashioned, David, and I love that about you. But let me treat this time ... please?" He finally consented, and drove me to town. He stopped at the curb in front of the Grill, directly behind a Mercedes convertible with the top down. A tall elderly gentleman was helping his round little lady into the passenger seat.

"How 'bout that?" David said, as he stuck his head out the window and yelled. "Hey, Tom, where do you think you're going?"

Tom Trippy looked up and laughed.

Lois giggled, climbed out of her seat and met us at the curb. She and I hugged, as women often do.

Tom and David slapped each other on the arms and laughed at who knows what.

The Trippys agreed to go back inside and have a cup of coffee with us. We ordered lunch and coffee for our friends from our table near the bar where several people watched a game of golf on the big screen. David occasionally swiveled his head around, trying to catch an exciting putt.

Tom pulled a flask out of his shirt pocket and poured a little hooch into his coffee.

Lois sipped her coffee quietly.

"Where's that wonderful dog of yours, Josephine?" Tom asked.

"He's at home, working ... taking care of Bratworse...."

"Bratworse? What's a Bratworse?"

"A monster kitten with multiple personalities ... most of them bad." I held out my wrists full of scratch marks as proof. Instantly, my neck tightened, and I wished I hadn't said anything negative about the little guy on the off chance someone might want to adopt him.

Our conversation bounced from sports to local burglaries to my work at the rink to new cars. Lois talked about their new convertible, saying that their old trade-in was a wreck.

I asked Tom if he knew about the underground safe. He shook his head, saying he built the rink, collected his pay and got out of there. He poured fresh hooch into his coffee refill.

"Wait; I just remembered something," Tom said. "We made this big hole in the wall for a door into a storage area. I think I remember seeing an old metal door from a bank safe propped against the wall down there, but we left the job before he did anything with it."

"Did you know Mario was a photographer?"

"No, he never mentioned it, but he wasn't a talker. It was like he was an observer, the kinda guy who's never really in the group. Ya know what I mean?"

Lois giggled, and wrapped her puffy hand over

Tom's hairy fingers. She talked about the weather, a trip to Tahiti they were planning and their bridge club partners—a couple she called "the Brainless Bauers."

"Bauer?" I mumbled. "I know a Bauer, but I don't know his first name."

"Well, Richard is an attorney—patent, I believe. His bridge partner is his young secretary, Fran, who he actually married last year." She rolled her eyes and leaned toward my ear, put a hand to her thin lips and whispered, "Fran's too young for him—about your age, Josephine, but she's heavy."

"Your Bauer friend has to be the same man that I'm thinking of—tall, thinning grey hair, hearing aid, has an office in Santa Cruz on the east side?"

"Oh, I never noticed the hearing aid, but yes, that's the one," she said, as she unconsciously patted Tom's hand. His hand turned over and squeezed hers. I noticed that Lois giggled less and less as she became more comfortable in the conversation.

I imagined David at Tom's age with me by his side. It was easy to picture and pleasant to think about.

David stared at my silly grin, and winked.

Tom laughed, and gulped down the last of his second refill. "I can see you young people want to be alone."

David swallowed a bite of turkey sandwich. "Hey, old buddy, it's OK. We like your company." But that didn't stop Tom and Lois from standing up to leave. We watched through the window as she took the driver's seat. Tom was still buckling his safety belt when Lois whipped a U-ee in the middle of the road, and pointed the convertible toward Prunedale.

David put his hand on mine. "Josie, what's the deal about a safe at the rink?"

I rubbed my neck. "Chester found a safe when he was exploring the tunnel—you know, the tunnel Tom built. No one knows the combination, so we have no idea what's in it."

"From what I've heard so far, this Portello guy was probably a miser. Maybe the safe is full of gold," David laughed.

I tried to picture Mario wearing a face like Jack Benny's, counting piles of gold coins. It didn't compute. A safe full of photographs and camera equipment would be more like it. Mr. Portello was a good businessman, but I never got the feeling he was obsessed with making money; after all, the lease agreements he was pushing were a couple decades late. Most business rentals in the twenty-first century involved a lease.

My thoughts drifted from Mario over to Alicia. I needed to talk to her, try to explain.

"David, please excuse me for a minute. I'm going outside to call Alicia." I left the dining room, walked across the patio full of lunchers and down the sidewalk another half-a-block for privacy. I dialed my best friend's number.

"Jo, are you all right? Your garbled messages last night didn't make sense."

Wow, she was worried, not angry. "Allie, I want to explain about last night. Someone I thought was guilty of murder packed up his car with suitcases. I saw him getting ready to leave and I couldn't just let him get away...."

"Of course not," Alicia said, dryly.

"So I followed him all the way into the Oakland hills ... to some little town. Anyway, it was a false alarm so I drove home. I hope you got a ride home."

"That's it? A false alarm? What does that mean?"

"I'd rather tell you in person," I said, feeling guilty of serious neglect. "I sort of forgot about you until I got to the summit and then it was too late to turn around.

I'm so sorry, Allie. What can I say?"

"For starters, you and David can come over for dinner tonight so that we can talk this over. I'd like to hear the details."

"Actually, David only knows that we went to the roller derby...."

"OK, Jo, come over anyway. I won't tell him," she sighed.

"You're wonderful, Allie. Thanks."

"Does that mean you're coming over? I made tamales."

Even before I told Alicia we would be there for dinner, much of the tightness in my neck had disappeared. I smiled at all the patrons sitting on the patio eating lunch, as I made my way back to David. I decided to tell my "chasing Grady" story to him in hopes that the rest of my tension would go away.

Good thing I never aspired to be a psychologist. My theory stunk. After I spilled my guts, David said I had used bad judgment and had little regard for my friends. He thought my murder theory didn't hold up and said I should concentrate on domestic issues, like my job, housework and training Bratworse.

I was stunned. I didn't know whether to roll my eyes or cry salty puddles of tears.

I wished I had another ride home, one without a lecture. Eventually, we ran out of words and the car was quiet except for golf news from the radio. I conveniently forgot to tell David that he was invited to the Quintanas for dinner. But I did tell him I had a headache. I wasn't lying. The pain traveled upward from my stiff neck and pushed at the back of my eyeballs like a paddle pounding ping-pong balls. I figured it was just-payment for not treating my friends decently.

David and I had been neighbors and friends for years

and "close friends" for the last two years without a single ugly word between us. Some dates were more exciting than others, but every date was with my special guy.

After seeing David's other side, I wondered how Solow could love him so much. How could I have fallen for someone who didn't believe in me and thought my values were silly. I enjoyed all the typical girl stuff, like flowers, dancing, movies, plays, trips and friends. But, unlike David, Alicia and most of my friends, I was driven to seek justice wherever it didn't exist, wherever someone got the short end of the stick, like poor old Mario Portello. I didn't have a choice. The drive was in my DNA.

My father's father, Grandpa Carl had worked as an Oakland policeman until the year I graduated from high school—the year he died from a heart attack. Everyone knew that Benjamin Carl persevered, always finding the bad guys and enough proof to put them in prison. I loved and admired my grandpa, and the city of Oakland was ever grateful for Lieutenant Carl.

I figured the justice gene came from Grandpa. I smiled a sad little smile, remembering him, missing him and wondering if I could learn to ignore the need for justice and let the proper officials do their job.

Even as David and I said a stiff goodbye, and gravel sprayed from his tires, I had already decided to let go of the Portello mystery. I would back off and try to act like a normal fifty-year-old woman. I would show off my mothering skills by potty training Bratworse. Once David saw how normal I was he would come crawling back to me, and then I would decide if he was worth keeping.

My eyes stung and my heart ached. The reality was I couldn't imagine not having David by my side.

I spent an hour on the Internet looking up the best

ways to train a kitten. First off, I would train him to do his business in a litter box, even though I had never actually caught him making puddles in the house. I used a steak knife to cut a cardboard box down to size and poured a layer of potting soil in the bottom. I set the makeshift litter box on the floor against the kitchen wall, a couple feet from the back door.

Over and over, I set the kitten in the box, but as soon as I let go, he always jumped out and ran to the door. Finally, I let Solow and Bratworse out. I watched as they ran to Solow's favorite spot just beyond the patio. And did their business!

I smacked my forehead with the palm of my hand. Solow had already taught the kitten to do his duty outside. I immediately dumped the potting soil into an empty clay pot and put the cardboard in the trash, feeling like a moronic make-believe mother.

As I paced the kitchen, it occurred to me that I might get to David's heart through his stomach with a favorite cookie recipe. My idea should have worked, but when I pulled the tray of cookies out of the oven, I was just a couple minutes late due to a phone call from Alicia. She had called to see if I had ice cream to go with her apple pie.

I tried scraping the black off each little arm and leg, but the gingerbread people fell apart in a crumbly mess.

I glanced at the clock, realizing I was already late for dinner at Alicia's. I fed the boys, stuffed a half-gallon of vanilla ice cream into a thermo-bag, grabbed my purse and drove my truck to Watsonville. The road looked blurry as I blinked and wiped my tears away. I finally got a grip on my emotions as I walked up to the front door of the lake house.

I rang the bell and seconds later Trigger threw the door open and led me to the kitchen where Alicia was filling a platter with tamales.

"Jo, honey, what's the matter? Where's David?"

My emotional control dissolved in an instant.

Ernie stepped into the room and immediately back-stepped out the door.

Even though Alicia was fifteen years younger, she knew how to console me. We hugged. I cried. She talked, and the tamales cooled. When I ran out of tears, the hiccups took over with unpredictable force.

The Quintana family acted like everything was normal as we settled into our chairs around the table and began passing platters of food.

I wondered what David was having for dinner.

"Jo ... hello, Jo, pass the salad please," Alicia said.

I hiccupped and passed the bowl. "The tamales are ... hic ... wonderful, Allie." The roller derby subject never came up. Instead, the Quintanas rallied around me, made me laugh, and filled my heart with their generous spirit.

CHAPTER TWELVE

Monday morning I dragged myself out of bed only because I had the key to the rink and people depended on me. The only other person who could unlock the door for my crew was Ralph, and his hours were unpredictable to say the least. Sometimes I wondered if he took ownership seriously. I quickly reminded myself that it wasn't my business. Mine was to paint and not get involved with other people's shortcomings, traits, suspicious activities or problems.

Robotically, I performed my daily shower and brushed my teeth, hair, whatever. I forced myself to live in the moment as I creamed, plucked, powdered and sprayed my way to hollow beauty. Who cared what I looked like? The red puffy eyes and sad posture would hopefully improve as the day progressed.

I shared my breakfast with Solow and Bratworse. They enjoyed it. I didn't taste a thing. I drank my cup of coffee because I always did. I fed the boys, filled their water bowls and drove to Santa Cruz, wondering the whole way how long a person can live with a fractured heart.

The mural was eighty percent finished. We would complete the project no later than Wednesday. After that, I would be working on the faux wood counter project by myself. I planned to use acrylic paints, layering the colors, brushing on the paint, combing the grain and knotholes and then an elegant marble finish on the counter top. Once all the paint was dry, I planned to add two coats of clear finish for depth and protection. Four or five half-days were all I needed.

Alicia greeted me at the back door to the rink. We grabbed paint supplies from the back of my truck and entered the building. Looking across the giant hall, we saw a long plastic banner affixed to a rafter fifteen feet above the counter. Its black and blue lettering advertized a roller derby competition coming to the rink on Memorial Day weekend.

Alicia gave me a look that said, "Forget it. I'm never going to a roller derby with you again!" Her eyes looked into mine. "Jo, everything is going to be all right. Trust me."

"He hates me...."

"Jo, you don't know any such thing. I know David, and I know he could never hate you. He doesn't understand you sometimes, but he still cares and he worries about you. He's a lot like your mom and me. He just wants to keep you safe."

"You're right, Allie, and I've decided to let go of Mario's murder. I'll show David that I'm just a regular gal, full of fun." I sniffed and wiped my eyes as we laid the tarps on the floor and unpacked paint supplies.

Kyle arrived carrying two ladders.

"Jo, what happened to you?" he asked as he positioned the ladders under the stretch of windows.

Alicia elbowed his skinny rib and handed him a paintbrush. We painted in silence until noon. Just as we were about to break for lunch, Ashley stopped by on her way back from "G's" to show us pictures of her beagle puppy. She handed me her smart phone and dragged a finger through a zillion pictures, stopping at a perky beagle pup wearing a silver collar.

"He's adorable. How long have you had him?"

Alicia and Kyle crowded in behind me for a look.

"We got Freddie two weeks ago today. We had pick-of-the-litter because Ralph knows the breeder," she snapped her gum. "Sometimes I think the whole world knows Ralph."

"So you got Freddie on Monday or Tuesday?"

"Let's see, Ralph flew home Monday and picked him up Tuesday. He wanted first pick and he got it. Freddie is bigger than all his brothers and sisters. It's like a miracle," she swooned. "We plan to send him to school—you know, make him sit and speak and stuff. See ya later."

We watched as Ashley's designer jeans sashayed across the room. She turned and waved goodbye from the open back door. Parked near the door was her Black Mercedes.

"OK, guys, lunch break." I dropped my brush in water and walked with my friends to the noodle place on the corner. On the way back to the rink, I waved at Grady through the large front window. He had Bonnie in the chair, giving her spiky yellow hair a trim. I didn't understand the style, but I didn't have to wear it either. There were lots of things I didn't understand, like Ralph supposedly coming back early from Hawaii because of Mario's murder, when he was already here picking out the plumpest puppy.

All afternoon, my mind kept wandering off to Hawaii. I pictured Ashley sitting on the beach all alone with her perfect figure stuffed into a tiny bikini, as her husband flew home in first class with a glass of wine and nothing but "big puppy" on his mind. Eventually, I was able to force my thoughts away from Hawaii, Ashley and Ralph. It was none of my business what idiotic things people did. I just needed to concentrate on painting ... oops!

"Allie, hand me a wet towel...." I said from five rungs up the ladder.

"At least you didn't spill paint on the floor," she chuckled, and handed up a wet cotton rag.

The black Mercedes had caught my attention just

before I spilled black paint down one pant leg while teetering on the fifth rung of the eight-foot ladder. What did it matter whether Ashley drove a Mercedes or Ralph a BMW? Both black. Why should I care what she and Ralph drove? All I cared about was cold black paint seeping through denim onto my leg.

I decided the rag wasn't enough and scrambled down the ladder and over to the ladies' restroom. Using wet paper towels, I sopped up the gooey paint and then dried everything with more paper towels. It took a lot of soap and water to bring back the original skin color to my hands. The leg would have to wait for a good soak in the tub.

I decided to check out the new office while I was on the west side of the building. Chester had stayed late, installing a door jam. Carpet, a door and a desk, and the room would be finished.

"Hi, Chester; looks like your job is just about finished."

Chester stood up. "Yep, how's your project coming along?"

"The walls are ninety percent done. I start a faux finish on the counter...."

"I mean your other project—who murdered Mario?"

"Wow, you think it was murder too? I mean, I'm not really working on that any more. I just don't have time."

"Yeah, and I'm the king of Denmark. What are you talking about, Josephine? You're not a quitter...."

"Yes, I am. I just can't...."

"Josephine, what's the matter with you? You're good at this. I was going to tell you that Bauer was here asking me questions while you guys went to lunch. He knows about the tunnel; said Bonnie told him. He seems pretty happy that there won't be a lease after all because his wife spends too much money."

"What does Mr. Bauer drive?" I asked before I could stop myself.

"I don't know, but if you're thinking it might be a certain black vehicle, don't forget, anyone can rent a car." He bent down and shot a couple of finishing staples into the trim.

"What about Fran? What did she think of Mr. Portello?"

"Do you know Fran?" Chester asked.

"I know about her—that's all. I know she married Richard Bauer."

"See, you're good at this stuff, Josephine. Don't be a quitter." Chester shoved the staple gun into his belt and wished me luck. Luck with what I wasn't sure. He headed out the front door, and I went back to my painters. We packed up our paint and equipment and left the rink.

I drove to the grocery store in Watsonville. Number one and two on my grocery list were cat food and Solow's kibble. I tossed the cans and kibble into the cart, grabbed a loaf of sour dough, a dozen eggs and half a gallon of ice cream, then scanned the produce aisle wondering if I needed anything green.

"The strawberries are pretty good today," a voice followed me.

I turned around to find Robert holding two little baskets of strawberries for me to inspect.

"Thanks, Robert." My mindless shopping was almost done. I tossed a pineapple and two potatoes into the shopping cart and headed for the checkout. Robert opened his register and rang up everything.

"Josephine, it's none of my business, but...."

"I'm fine, Robert, just tired."

"Uh-huh." He turned his eyes up to a twirling fan attached to the ceiling.

Customers lined up behind me so I helped Robert by

bagging everything and carted my groceries out to the truck. Somehow I made it home, but I didn't remember driving. My mind was fixed on a misunderstanding with a guy named David. I barely thought about Ralph and his new puppy. It wasn't my problem.

It was almost six-thirty when I rolled up the driveway, unloaded the groceries and fed my starving dog and kitten. Solow had a new claw mark across his nose. Hopefully I would be able to teach him to be assertive and stand up to the little brat. We didn't need another Fluffy-Solow situation where my dog regularly gets his ego kicked into the next county.

Bratworse looked innocent as he gorged himself on milk. As soon as I picked him up, he fell asleep in my hand. I placed him on his bed and began my own food binge. I guess that's what you'd call it—ice cream for dinner.

I washed down the ice cream with a cup of tea and a chocolate bar, adding guilt to my sadness. It had been sixteen years since I sat around feeling sorry for myself … not since I lost my husband to the drunk driver of an eighteen-wheeler.

I checked the answering machine and my emails— nothing from David. I thought about calling him, but Ms. Pride, the stubborn, old-fashioned female forever lodged in my head, had wrapped my tongue in a knot. She would die before she would let me call David. What would I say to him anyway? I wasn't about to apologize for anything he thought was odd behavior on my part.

The phone rang. I jumped. My heart pounded as I picked up the receiver. It rang two more times as I placed reading glasses on my nose and read the name in the little window. Heat radiated north, all the way to my sweaty brow. The caller was … David Galaz. I decided to let it ring a couple more times before I pushed the talk button. Maybe he would think I was busy—had a life and friends. Just as I pressed "talk," the line went silent.

I slammed the phone down, and Solow cringed.

"I'm sorry big guy. I'm not upset with you." I dropped a little scoop of ice cream in his bowl and helped myself to another couple of scoops with strawberries, still hating myself for not answering the phone. What if David wanted to be with me? I could do that. I don't hold grudges. But the phone didn't ring again all evening.

I put on the ten o'clock news and promptly fell asleep on the sofa.

A faraway ringing sound jarred my brain, but my body felt glued to the floor. I stretched my arms out, trying to reach my purse with the cell phone in it. A tall woman wearing a red dress reached my purse first, took out the phone and answered it. Her voice sounded like mine when she said, "Oh, David darling, it's you."

I struggled even harder to reach the phone. I wanted to talk to David, but I couldn't move and the lady in red acted like she knew him and told him I wasn't home.

Suddenly, the front door flew open and David marched in holding a cell phone to his ear. He walked right past me as if I didn't exist—straight to the yellow-haired woman holding my phone to her ear. They talked to each other over the phone, ignoring me completely.

Solow barked at the woman.

I recognized Bratworse even though he was a full-grown cat. He and his many furry cousins spat and clawed at my poor dog. Solow growled at the cats and whimpered when they ganged up on him.

Finally, I was able to move closer to the fracas. I looked for David but didn't see him anywhere.

Suddenly, Bratworse leaped onto Solow's back, clawing and roaring like the big Hollywood lion just before a movie starts.

Solow howled in agony, his feelings hurt beyond repair.

Ms. Red picked up her fifty-pound purse and swung it at my cat. Bratworse flew across the room like a furry baseball headed for centerfield. I looked to see where he was going and realized I was at the "Bowl & Bowl" bowling alley. The cat landed on top of ten pins and a very fast bowling ball was streaking down the lane.

I heard cat screams.

The woman in red laughed.

I tried to tackle her but my foot was caught in the strap of her heavy red purse.

Somewhere a phone was ringing.

Sadly, all that was left of the cat was his collar.

The nightmare seemed so real and stayed with me for a long time after I woke up. I finally trundled down the hall and climbed into bed with eyes wide-open, brain spinning. I concentrated on listening to Solow's breathing, wondering how he could fall asleep so easily. But that was all I remembered as I fell into a dreamless sleep.

CHAPTER THIRTEEN

Tuesday blues sounded like the name of a country song—sad and hopeless. I lay in bed remembering the "lady in red" nightmare, doing a reenactment in my head of poor Bratworse flying through the air, landing on the pins, only to be slammed by a speeding bowling ball. I turned my head and looked across the room at Solow in his doggie bed. He was alone. I started to wonder if the kitten really was smashed by a bowling ball.

Somebody purred.

I followed the purr and found Bratworse cuddled into my armpit. What a relief. But my brain could not shake the nightmare. It hung around making me wonder who was the woman in red, and what the dream meant. I was used to having vivid, sometimes scary dreams in Technicolor, and usually they had something to do with my life. The fact that David had ignored me was just like reality. But who was the yellow-haired woman and why did she murder my cat?

I rolled out of bed with Bratworse in one hand and let him out the back door with Nurse Solow following just inches behind. I watched them for a moment, but my eyes moved toward the knoll between my house and David's. I couldn't see his house because of the uneven terrain, but if he had a fire in the fireplace, I would see the smoke. No smoke that Tuesday. Even the sun was absent, hiding behind grey clouds.

By the time I reached Ralph's Roller Rink, I had successfully forced the Bowl and Bowl nightmare from my mind. Alicia left her car and greeted me with her usual perky countenance, as she helped carry paint supplies into the building. We began our last day of painting the Hokey Pokey song.

Kyle arrived looking happy that it was payday, dropping little hints like "My rent's overdue."

"Don't worry, Kyle, I have the checks right … ah … maybe I didn't put them in my purse. I'll just go get them on our lunch break," I said as I riffled through my purse for a second time. The extra trip home, the time sitting in traffic, the wasted gasoline—none of those thoughts put me in a bad mood. My mood had already hit bottom. I had quit caring, except that Kyle and Alicia were entitled to their money.

"Jo, why don't you call David? I'm sure he would be happy to…."

"No. He wouldn't be happy to bring the checks. I'm the idiot who forgot them. I'll get them myself. In fact, I'm going right now. I'm sorry, Allie, I don't feel good." I closed my purse and hurried to the back door, tears stinging my eyes, ready to break loose.

I opened the back door, staring straight into the morning sun. Blinking back tears, I walked to my truck. Next to it was a sporty little red car with a long-legged woman climbing out of the driver's seat. She turned her head my way and slammed the door.

"Jo? Josephine Carl … is that you?" she asked.

"Oh my gosh, … Franny? I haven't seen you since the senior prom when you and Ted got caught on the fire escape … ah, it's been a long time. How are you?" We gave each other a hug that included air-kisses and pats on the back.

Fifty pounds overweight with too much makeup and hair dye, Fran looked older than her fifty years. Dark circles under her eyes and thinning hair didn't help.

"I'm fine. I work here with my husband, Richard. He's a patent attorney, you know. How are you, Jo?"

"Just fabulous," I lied. "My last name is Stuart now. I'm a widow, but I have a wonderful, ah, fiancé."

"What are you doing in this neighborhood?" she asked, her blue eyes examining my very unglamorous paint-smeared outfit.

"My painters and I are finishing up a mural right here at the rink. I was just about to drive out to my home in Aromas," I smiled. It hurt to smile, but I did it. Pretty soon I was smiling for real, realizing my life wasn't so bad, just temporarily de-railed. I regretted the lie about having a fiancé, but it was too late to retract it.

Three years in a row, Fran and I had attended the same high school art classes. She was awarded a scholarship to UCSC. I attended Community College. My love of art became my passion and my provider. Fran told me she dropped out of college, worked as a model in LA, and married a movie director. When the marriage ended and her looks matured, she moved back to Santa Cruz and married Richard.

"How's your family? Do they still live in Santa Cruz?" I asked.

"Mom's in a half-way house, my brother moved to Kenya with a twenty-year-old gypsy and my dad died years ago."

"Oh," I gulped.

"Let's do lunch sometime," she said, twirling a long strand of coppery hair.

"Sure, I'd love to." Someday when I had nothing better to do.

I climbed into my ridiculously uncool truck and watched Fran enter the patent office from the back door. If I had still been interested in the Mario murder, I would have asked Fran a few questions, like, "Where were you the day Mr. Portello was run over?" For a minute, I was glad I didn't have to think of an old friend as a possible suspect, until I remembered how competitive we were in class, and how she had accidentally spilled ink on my best ever still-life drawing in the tenth grade.

Compared to Fran, my life was good. I had no wrinkles, grey hair or health issues. I had many interests besides painting and detective work, although none came to mind.

All of a sudden, I realized my depression was lifting. I felt my appetite coming back so I motored over to Taco Bell for a mid-morning bite to eat. I sat at a glued-to-the-concrete table-bench contraption on the patio with a soda and three tacos watching traffic go by. Nothing like a little hot sauce to get those endorphins fired up.

I was still comparing my life to Fran's when I saw a black Miata like David's whiz by with a woman in the passenger seat. My neck snapped to the right and my jaw dropped to the floor when I saw the license. It was his. "OFF 2 OTIS" it read!

Anger in the form of prickly heat spread over my body until I thought I would burst into flames. A lump grew in my throat, half-choking me as it extinguished my appetite. How could he take up with another woman so soon? What did she have that I didn't? She looked young and blond—probably a cheap bimbo.

Suddenly, it occurred to me there was no reason not to investigate Mario's murder. David had dumped me so I might as well ignore his wishes and live my life using my natural talents and interests. My anger surged. How dare he try to stifle me!

I almost never throw food away—only old containers of leftovers covered with green fur. But seeing another woman riding with David was more than I could handle. I tossed—slammed actually—two and a half tacos into the garbage with a grunt, leaving the opening flap swinging noisily. A group of teens at the next table looked worried, like I might moon them or commit a random act of violence.

I fired up my truck and headed south. Halfway home, I ran out of tears. I had finally gained control over my emotions, I thought. I motored up Otis, and glanced at David's Miata in his driveway. I figured she was in his house. The lump grew in my throat again. I tried to greet Solow but I could only grunt. He and Bratworse followed me into the house. I gave them brunch, grabbed the checks and hurried back to the rink.

Alicia and Kyle were taking their lunch break when I walked in. I studied the mural for a moment and handed over their checks.

"Obviously, we're in the last couple hours of this project. I think it turned out well, and I want to thank you two for the terrific work you did. I will be back later today to pick up the equipment...."

"Jo, you're leaving again? I mean, don't worry, we can finish up here—no sweat."

"Yeah, like we can finish in one or two hours." Kyle looked puzzled, but that was nothing new.

"Thanks for understanding...." I said as I turned and walked toward the back door. I already knew where I was going. Mom would fix me a cup of tea and tell me about her rose club party, and I would forget to be so sad for a while.

As it turned out, Myrtle stopped by and had tea with us. We sat at the breakfast bar in the kitchen while Dad watched TV in the den.

"Sweetheart, your eyes look a little red. Are you getting enough sleep?" Mom asked.

"Dear, are you sure you're all right?" Myrtle chimed in.

"Yeah, I'm fine; guess I need more sleep. My new kitten keeps me up at night," I lied. I wasn't ready to give up on David completely. Even though things were looking pretty grim, I was unable to imagine myself without David, and unwilling to talk to anyone about him, not even my own mother. I sipped tea and ate a piece of Mom's banana bread. She didn't like to bake, but she hated to throw away over-ripe bananas, and the recipe she had used for the last half-century made her look like another Julia Child.

Mom went to the den to see if Dad wanted tea and banana bread.

"Myrtle, you know lots of people. Do you know Fran and Richard Bauer in the patent office next door to Bonnie's Bingo Parlor?" I reached for another piece of banana bread.

"No, dear. Is it important?"

I leaned closer. "It is important. I'm trying to figure out who murdered Mario Portello. Shush, Mom's coming back."

Myrtle giggled.

"Did I miss a joke?" Mom asked as she poured a cup of tea for Dad and cut a slice of her famous bread.

We looked at her with blank expressions.

Mom shrugged, loaded a tray and carried it down the hall to the den.

Myrtle understood my need for secrecy and kept her voice low. "I know Mario's neighbor, Nicki Waller. She's my niece's best friend, and she hated Mario with every bone in her overly muscled body."

"That name sounds familiar. Why did she hate him?" My heart did a double thud.

"About a month ago, someone poisoned her two little fox terriers. Actually, they belonged to her good-for-nothing son. Nicki swore it was Mario who poisoned them. My niece said that Mr. Portello was shouting at Nicki and her son just two days before the dogs were found dead. Mario had threatened to strangle the yappy little noise-makers if she didn't shut them up."

"Shut who up, Myrtle?" Mom asked as she rejoined us.

"Oh, dear, I forgot what we were talking about," Myrtle said, fidgeting with her fork and a few rogue bread crumbs.

"Mom, your banana bread tastes extra good today." I had been eating the same bread from the same recipe since she baked her first loaf for my tenth birthday party. I was the only kid around who had a flaming loaf of banana bread for a birthday cake. But I preferred that over Mom's saggy, off-kilter cakes.

"Same old recipe, dear," she smiled. "Are you not working today?"

"We're finishing up the mural. In fact, I have to get back to the rink before three. That's when the skaters invade the place. Chester did a nice job of rebuilding the office so Ralph decided to open up for business. I'll be fauxing the counter starting tomorrow."

"What will it look like, Josephine, when the counter is finished?" Myrtle asked.

"Like redwood on three sides and a slab of marble on top. Why don't you stop by, Myrtle, and see our mural … when you're in the neighborhood, that is?"

Mom cocked her head to one side. "In the neighborhood?"

Myrtle gave me a look that said, "Leola doesn't know I gamble."

"I just thought if you or Myrtle happened to be on the east side of town sometime, I would love to show you around the rink." I stood up and said goodbye to Mom and Myrtle, walked to the den and kissed Dad goodbye. He snorted and woke himself up.

"Dad, now that you're awake…."

"I was just resting my eyes, dear. Looks like you

should too."

"I'm fine, Daddy. I was just wondering about your friend, Mr. Waller, and why he wants to shut down the rink."

Dad stood up. "Sweetheart, what makes you think that? He's just doing his job."

"Does he have a temper?"

"He has a much younger wife and she has a scrappy, loser son. The kid can't keep a job no matter what, in and out of jail—you know what I mean. Sometimes I don't know how old Waller handles it all."

I hugged my dad goodbye and scampered out to the truck, climbed in and drove across town to the rink, mulling over the Waller family dynamics as I drove.

It was two o'clock when I arrived. My painters had already left and the mural was obviously finished. I signed the painting with "Wildbrush Murals" in the far lower-right-hand corner in small letters, feeling like it was not my most memorable mural. I hauled ladders, paints and other equipment out to the truck. As I tossed the last canvas bag into the bed and pulled the top down, I heard a voice and turned.

Bonnie took a long drag on her cigarette and pushed the smoke out her nose.

"Josephine, are you finished over here?"

"Not really; I'll be back tomorrow...."

"Have you seen Ralph's puppy yet?"

"No, just a picture...." I opened the driver's side door.

"Looks like Ralph was in town the day Mario bought the farm," she said.

"Yeah, but he didn't have anything against Mr. Portello, did he?"

"The way I see it, Ralph wanted to up-grade, make lots of changes, but Mario was in charge of the finances and wouldn't let go of the money. The old man acted like he still owned the place. I walked in on a shouting match. As soon as they saw me, Mario ducked back into his little office and Ralph acted like nothing happened." She took another drag and tossed the butt.

"Thanks for sharing, Bonnie. To tell you the truth, I'm getting nowhere. I have half a dozen suspects, but no silver bullet, as they say. Just a bunch of birdshot." I climbed into the driver's seat and headed for home, more perplexed than ever.

CHAPTER FOURTEEN

Wednesday morning arrived. Streams of light filtered into my bedroom, forcing me into consciousness, causing me to face another day without David.

Solow greeted me with his wet nose on my cheek as usual.

I opened my eyes and looked around. Bratworse was missing. I leaped out of bed and kicked my feet into slippers.

"Meow."

I heard a familiar cry and looked around expecting to see Bratworse hanging from the drapes or a lampshade.

"Meow."

Following the sound of his cries, I lifted my blanket and picked up the little yellow fuzz-ball. His motor revved like a B-29 bomber. He must have spent the night under the covers at the end of the bed. I checked my toes for scratches. Not a mark! I carried Brat to the kitchen and let him outside with Solow.

After a quick breakfast, I searched the tool shed for a sea sponge, a couple goose feathers, sandpaper and a jar of clear coat—essentials for my faux wood and marble project at the rink. Over the years, I had taught myself how to create fake wood and stone through experimentation. My house was full of fauxed lamps, tables and flowerpots, not to mention the items I passed on to Mom, Myrtle and Aunt Clara.

I was on the wrong end of the old saying, "timing is everything." After years of experimenting with paint, learning my craft, artisans began offering free lessons on the Internet. They demonstrated everything one needed to know about faux, removing all the mystery and possibility of disaster.

It was eight-thirty by the time all my domestic chores were completed, truck loaded and pets fed. Traffic was light until Aptos where the usual slow-and-go began. It was almost nine-thirty when I parked at the rink and hauled my canvas bag full of paints and supplies into the building.

I found Ralph and Chester in the new office standing opposite each other with the trapdoor between them. They looked up when I wished them a good morning.

"Mornin,' Josephine. We have a decision to make." Chester eyed Ralph. "Whether to carpet over this trap door, or leave a hole in the carpet and cover it with a rug."

"Cover it with a rug has my vote," I said, since my curiosity was anything but satisfied.

Ralph rubbed his chin. "What about you, Chester?"

"I vote for the rug." He grinned at me. "I'm still curious about that big old safe."

"You're right. There might be something in it. Go ahead and cut a hole." Ralph grimaced at the thought of defacing his new red carpet, but I knew he was smiling inside at the thought of a safe full of riches.

I felt the presence of someone standing behind me, and turned. "Good morning, Grady," I said to the man wearing a rumpled button-down shirt and bloodshot eyeballs. I wanted to ask about his Grandma but not in front of other people.

"Yes, I guess it is a good morning," he mumbled.

"Hey, Grady, how would you like to help us open the safe?" Ralph asked.

"Sure, I'll go down and see what we're up against." He squeezed himself through the hole, crept down the ladder and shouted back, "They used the door to an old bank vault, Hercules, actually, with a combination lock—simple if we had the combination." Grady popped his head up to tell us he would need his instruments. He climbed out of the hole and brushed dust off his black pants.

Grady seemed to be in a hurry to get back to his shop. As he pushed open one of the double entrance doors, he said he would bring his tools to the rink the next day, if he didn't have to go out of town.

I figured "out of town" probably meant, funeral. Poor Grady.

The front door swung shut and instantly opened again. Celeste entered, her thinning yellow hair back-lit by the sunny outdoors. Her tight jeans and jeweled blouse looked like they came from G's, but the young style didn't bless her with a youthful look. The closer she came to us the closer to seventy-something she looked.

"I stopped by to see the mural," she said. "I heard something about a safe. Is it true there's a big old safe in this place?" Her eyes searched the three of us one at a time, ending with Ralph. "We missed you and Ashley at the funeral."

Ralph was quick to apologize. "Sorry, Celeste, something came up...."

"Yes, I'm sure," she snarked.

"We found a safe, all right, but so far we haven't been able to open it." Ralph pointed to the obvious hole in the floor.

Celeste stiffly bent forward to inspect the ladder and a smidgen of tunnel. She wanted to know if we had found anything else down there. None of us offered an answer to the question, so she moved on to the mural wall, oohing and aahing a bit before she tramped her four-inch heels out the front door to her black Caddie parked at the curb.

"All she wants is an inheritance, but I'm betting Mario didn't give her a dime in his will," Ralph said, as soon as the woman was out of the building.

"How do you know that?" I asked.

"She was always coming down here to the rink, bugging him for money. Her chances of getting anything are slim to nada."

"Did you tell Mario about the murals you were planning?"

"Sure did. He cracked up when I told him my idea of Hokey Pokey words across the wall. First time he was willing to go along with my plans and the first time I saw him laugh. Gotta run, you guys," Ralph said as he headed for the back entrance.

Chester unrolled a length of red carpet for the office while I removed everything from the near-by counter. Cash register, telephone and a bottle of hand sanitizer were stashed on the floor against the wall. I sanded the sides and top of the stationary structure, wiped it all down with damp rags and sanded it again. My little electric Black and Decker obliterated all other noises in the building.

From the corner of my eye, I saw something move. A uniformed officer stepped back from the wood dust, coughing into his sleeve. I unplugged my ancient sander and waved at the dusty air hoping to make breathing a little easier.

Fishburn coughed, "Excuse me, Ms. Stuart."

"Oh, hi, Sergeant, I was just finishing up here. What can I do for you?"

"I heard that you folks have a tunnel and a safe here at the rink. Mr. Rattini asked me to come by and inspect the tunnel to see if there might be something in it that could be connected to the murder."

"So you think it was murder?" I felt like saying "I told you so."

"I have a witness who saw a blond woman in a black car backing out of the hole in the wall. Apparently, she was walking up the sidewalk and was almost struck by the car. The witness said the woman was white, between thirty and sixty."

"I have at least four suspects who could be a match and with a blond wig, even more suspects," I said. "That was the best she could do for the age?"

"Yeah, well the description wasn't very good because the witness said there was so much debris on the windshield."

"Who is this witness?"

"A woman coming out of the barbershop. I'm conducting an investigation so I can't tell you her name."

The sergeant asked me to show him where the tunnel was located. I walked him over to the new little office, and watched him scrunch his shoulders together and stuff his body down the rabbit hole.

While I waited for the officer to resurface, Chester carried the rolled-up carpet into the office and dropped it beside the hole.

Fishburn heard the thump and popped his head up, looked around and climbed out.

"Not much down there. Has the safe been opened?" he asked.

"Nope. We're working on it," I said.

"I know a guy who might be able to help us." He brushed cobwebs off his uniform and asked me to go to coffee with him.

"Do what?" I stuttered. "Oh, coffee, that would be fine." I suddenly had coffee jitters and hadn't even been near the stuff since breakfast. We walked to a bagel shop around the corner, ordered coffee and bagels and sat at a table by the window. It was somewhere between breakfast and lunch, and we were the only customers in the place. The sergeant sat across from me, stirring cream into his coffee.

"Sergeant Fishburn, have you come up with any suspects or motives?"

"I can't respond to that, but like I said, I have an eye witness."

"I was an eye witness, but my statement wasn't taken seriously."

"Now, now, Ms. Stuart, you have to admit you were a bit unraveled that day."

"Yeah, maybe, but I saw what I saw." I wiped cream cheese from my chin with a napkin Fishburn handed me as he tapped his cleft chin with the other hand. I watched his electric blue eyes check to make sure my face was clean.

"Josephine, is there anything you would like to tell me about Mario's murder? You say you have four or more suspects. Do they have motives?"

"Well, there's Gianna, the wife, who didn't sleep in the same room with Mario, has no pictures of him around the house and isn't interested in his work at the rink. There's his stepsister who says Mario hated her, and she has no feelings at all for him, but would like to inherit some of his money." I paused for a moment.

"Any more?"

"There's Bonnie who rented from Mario and was angry about the lease idea, and says she hardly knew him even though she used to be a roller derby girl right here at the rink. There's Fran from the patent office next door who worried about the rent increase, and Ralph's wife Ashley who says she was in Hawaii at the time of the murder, even though Ralph was in Santa Cruz picking out a puppy."

"Anyone else?"

"Mario's neighbor, Nicki, claims he poisoned her son's two dogs. But she has dark brown hair. Actually,

Mario's wife Gianna's hair is black and Fran's is a coppery color. But someone might have worn a blond wig."

"Looks like you've done your homework," Fishburn said, as he scribbled in his notebook. "Would you like me to walk you back to the rink?"

"No. I'm sure you need to get back to work. But I would like to know if the witness said anything about the black car."

"Actually, we found a car two days ago in the surf, at the bottom of a cliff in Monterey County. It came from Experience Rental Group. No prints whatsoever. But some of the dents are being examined for paint specks, etc. We're pretty sure it's the car we've been looking for."

"So, you've been on the case ... ah, even when you thought it was just a senior moment and not a murder?"

"Some of the things you told me made sense, especially when we found the car."

"Thank you, Sergeant, for the coffee and bagel, and for sharing." I tried to look calm, but knowing the car was rented meant that any of my suspects could have committed murder.

The sergeant paid our bill and left through the back door. I sat for a moment feeling alone and empty. I stared out the window watching the traffic go by. I watched Grady drive to the corner in his black car and turn right—just like the night I followed him. His loneliness had to be much worse than mine. At least, I had my family and friends. The only thing I didn't have was David. I stood up and left the coffee shop.

Back at the rink, I was alone. Chester had gone to lunch. The place was too quiet—creepy quiet—like the quiet before a storm.

It was already noon when I finally started the faux finish. I began with a dabbing, smearing and squishing of paint, applied with a natural sea sponge. I randomly dipped into white, off-white, beige, a tad bit of grey and some extender, blending the different colors and shades, but not completely. When the counter was covered with paint end-to-end, I stood back, squinted and retouched a few spots.

The next process had to happen quickly before the paint had time to dry. I crumpled a plastic bag and pounced it over the painted surface, giving the marble another dimension. I worked fast, pouncing, stamping, smearing and twisting the plastic. When the pouncing was done, I ran my thumbnail through the paint creating white veins. Sweat ran down my face. I wiped it away with my shirtsleeve.

The two-foot-wide by six-foot-long counter was starting to look like a slab of marble. I let it dry for half an hour while I sat on a bench licking a tootsie-pop, thinking about a black car in the surf. On my way back to the counter project, I checked the office to see if the new carpet had been installed. It had. Maybe Chester would not be coming back. It looked like his job was finished.

I lifted the little rug and then the trapdoor. Why did I decide to climb down the ladder? Because it was there. The familiar earthy smell and dim lighting gave the place a humbleness that somehow comforted me. I felt like I was ten years old in my own hiding place, making up an adventure.

Suddenly, there was a far away rumble and the sound of creaking timbers. Dust filled the underground room as the floor moved side-to-side under my sandaled feet. I turned and grabbed hold of the ladder. An athletic ten-year-old could not have climbed it faster. Dust followed me to the top where I leaped out of the hole, panting. I had no heart for that kind of adventure.

There is nothing better than a creative project for forgetting about a little earthquake. Little earthquakes are sometimes precursors to "the big one." If they happen after a "big" earthquake, they are called aftershocks. After fifty years of living in earthquake country, I should have been immune.

The counter top was dry so I brought out my favorite goose feather and dipped the tip of the feather into watered-down Payne's grey paint. Because I am right-handed and my left hand is worse than uncoordinated, I held the feather in my left hand, turning it sideways and dragging it to create veins. The lines were thick and thin, smeared and crossing, all done with a shaky left hand. I added a few tiny dots and dashes, and the marble was done except for the clear coats which would be added another day.

I took a picture of the counter top and thought about sending it in an email to David. Dang! I promised myself I wouldn't think about him. Too late, so I spent my drive home thinking about special dates and wonderful times we had spent together.

I parked as usual in front of the house. Solow and the Brat were sleeping on the porch by the front door. They gave me a warm welcome. As we entered the house, the answering machine played the last couple of words from a voice that sounded like it might have been David. I reached to press the replay button; but at that same moment, Bratworse leaped onto the side table sending the answering machine to the floor with a crash. The old plastic recorder broke into five pieces and a tangle of tape—along with my hopes.

CHAPTER FIFTEEN

I was tempted to call in sick Thursday morning, claiming acute sadness and loss of energy. But I would have to call the boss and since I was the boss/owner of Wildbrush Murals, I told myself it would be easier to go to work without a fuss.

I took my time dressing and eating. No one was depending on me for the roller rink key. Chester had finished his job. At least the money I earned from the faux finish would be all mine. Maybe I would spend it on something wild and crazy—or not.

I picked up the phone and dialed David's number. After several rings, David's voice asked me to leave a message. What should I say? Why was I calling? I couldn't tell the truth—that I was lost without him. Finally, I opened my mouth to tell a lie and his answering service beeped. Time was up.

I dialed Alicia. She picked up right away, and I asked her to meet me at Charlie Hong Kong's noodle shop for lunch. She agreed and invited me to come to her house for dinner Friday night. I didn't commit to Friday dinner because even though Friday was only one day away, it seemed like centuries. Time had stopped for me. Even my faux work seemed to happen in slow motion. By noon, I had applied one round of clear coat over the faux marble and painted four sides of the counter with a burnt umber base color.

Just before noon, I locked up the rink and walked over to Charlie Hong Kong's on Soquel Avenue. I found Alicia sitting against the back wall on a long bench shared with other customers. She greeted me with a hug.

Ashley sat beside her, eating noodles smothered in shredded raw vegetables.

I sat down across the table from Alicia. She said she had ordered for both of us since we always wanted the chicken-pesto noodle bowl. Her number was called. I crossed the room to the pick-up counter, picked up the bowls and carried them to our table.

"Do you eat here often, Ashley?" I asked.

She nodded as she twirled noodles around her chopsticks and plunged them into her mouth. "I always eat here before I shop at G's across the street. It's so convenient, don't you think?"

"My philosophy has always been, don't eat anything before trying on tight little jeans."

"You're so funny, Josephine," she giggled.

"Did you guys feel the earthquake yesterday?"

No answer, just more slurping of noodles.

"It was a quick shake—only lasted a couple seconds...." I poked a twisted gob of noodles into my mouth. A few got away and attached themselves to my paint shirt.

"How's the faux finish coming along, Jo?" Alicia smiled. "Did you know you have noodles on your shirt?" The conversation seemed trivial and stilted with "third-party Ashley" sitting there, feeding her skinny little body.

"The faux should be finished by Tuesday, in plenty of time for Memorial Day weekend." I captured another clump of noodles with my chopsticks. "Ashley, how's the puppy? Have you named it yet?"

"We named him Freddie," she chuckled. "The name came to us the first time we saw him. Remember the dog named Freddie in that movie ... with what's-his-name playing the cop?"

Since we all experience senior moments, Alicia and I

nodded as if we understood what Ashley was saying. It sounded to me like Ralph and his wife had picked out the puppy together. So why had they pretended to still be in Hawaii? Were they ever in Hawaii?

"Now that my work is winding down," I looked at Ashley, "I'm thinking I might take a trip to Hawaii. Which island do you like the best?" I ignored Alicia's harsh look of disapproval.

"Oh, we like Maui," Ashley chirped.

"Where did you stay?"

"We always stay at the Maui Hilton."

"These noodles sure are good, aren't they Jo?" Alicia said as she reached across the table and plucked a couple wiggly runaways off my t-shirt. She knew I wasn't going to Hawaii any time soon. She knew I would pay my bills, put a little money away and start another mural job as soon as I could. Hawaii would have to wait.

Ashley finished her lunch, excused herself and sashayed across the street to G's.

Alicia scolded me for trying to finagle information out of Ashley and then pumped me about David, but stopped when she noticed a stoic but fragile smile pasted on my face. Speeding away from the David subject, she asked if she could see the roller rink tunnel.

I was more than happy to take Alicia on a tour of the tunnel, but once we were down the ladder, I found myself nervously listening for another earthquake. Fortunately, the place was as quiet as the grey dust covering the old oak desk and bentwood chair.

Alicia's eyes were big and darting all around.

"This is amazing," she sputtered. "It's like a time-capsule, like a museum. Didn't you say you found some pictures?"

I walked Alicia over to the desk and opened the drawer. She thumbed through the photos with a bland look on her face, except for the last picture.

"Whoa, look at this hairy little girl!"

"Yeah, and I think I know her." I closed the drawer and we took a few steps over to the ladder. "If only we could open the safe," I mumbled to myself. Grady had not been back to the rink. Maybe his shop was busy or he was out of town. We climbed the ladder and sucked in some fresh air. Alicia helped me position the trapdoor. I put the big brass key in the lock, turned it and returned the key to the Tootsie-pop jar on the top shelf.

Alicia asked about the faux finish. She had watched me replicate stones such as marble and granite before, but she wanted to know how I would create the look of redwood. I pointed out the dark brown already painted solidly on all three sides of the counter. She watched me mix up the next coat, much lighter than the original coat consisting of burnt sienna acrylic paint mixed with a little bit of extender.

Under the lip of the countertop, with a level in one hand and pencil in the other, I drew the lines that would define a four-inch by six-foot long strip of wood. Staying within the lines, I brushed on the glaze using a stiff three-inch throw-away type brush made with squirrel hairs, making sure not to cover the area solidly. Before the glaze had time to dry, I scraped a comb across the length of the plank. Using a corner of the comb, I swirled in a few knotholes in various sizes.

"Jo, it looks like wood!"

"That's the whole idea. I'll add a few more irregularities and highlights later. Now that you know how simple it is, you'll probably be my competition," I laughed.

"Not me. I'm happy painting murals on an irregular basis. By the way, when is the next job?"

"I mailed the sketches, but the starting date isn't

nailed down yet. It's a city-planner's thing. They probably have to vote on it so keep your fingers crossed." This was another example of the unreliability of my work, which made trips to Hawaii as common as monkeys on surfboards.

The back door slammed.

Ralph strolled toward us wearing khaki slacks and a colorful Hawaiian-print button-down shirt. He smiled when he saw the strip of faux wood.

"Looks like that was a good idea I came up with."

"Yes," I said, remembering how I had come up with the idea. "Nice shirt."

"Yeah, had it for years."

I felt Alicia's elbow in my side. "Pick up any new shirts this trip?"

"Not really; they don't make 'em like they used to."

I gave Alicia a squinty-eyed *I told you so.* "Guess you're happy that your rent isn't going up," I said to Ralph as he put his face down close to the marble finish, examining every aspect of it.

He jerked his head up. "What do you mean, rent going up?"

"I heard Mario was about to raise all the rents. I just assumed yours was included in the hike." I cocked my head, waiting for a reply.

"Now that you mention it, I think Mario did say something about a lease. I'm more of a promoter than a bookkeeper. I left that stuff to him."

"He could raise the rent and you wouldn't care?"

"Of course, I care; it's just that I have so many other things to worry about," he said as he turned and headed for the back door.

"He can't take the heat," I whispered.

"Jo, didn't you say that Sergeant Fishburn is on the case? Why don't you relax and let him sort it all out?"

"I'm not good at relaxing, you know that. When was

the last time you saw me relax?" It was true. Causes were what I lived for, and it was Mario's cause that kept me awake at night.

Alicia left me with my work. I finished glazing and combing the sides of the counter. All I needed to do was add highlights to the knotholes and a couple layers of clear coat. I decided to finish up Friday. I packed up my equipment, locked the doors and climbed into my truck. But I had no desire to be home, next door to the man who hated me, so I drove to the police department in downtown Santa Cruz looking for Fishburn.

I circled the police department four times, watched a van pull out from the curb and slipped my truck into the empty space. I dropped all my quarters into the parking meter and hoofed it down the sidewalk to the cobbled entry of the police station where a sign on the door read, "Closed Fridays, Saturdays and Sundays." Luckily, it was Thursday. Apparently crime was forbidden on those other days. I stepped into the small office containing four empty desks and one lady police officer working at a computer.

"Can I help you, ma'am?"

"I'm looking for Sergeant Fishburn...."

"Ma'am, most of our officers are on patrol or working on cases." She pushed a paper across her desk. "Fill this out and I'll see that he gets it."

"Thanks. Do you have a pen?"

She handed over a sharpie.

I fiddled with the form, stared out the window, but was unable to come up with the right words to express things I had learned from Ashley and Ralph having to do with Hawaii, the shirt and the puppy. My suspicions deserved to be handled with gravity. Finally I gave up and wrote a note for the sergeant to meet me at the rink Friday around noon.

I handed the paper to the policewoman who checked

it over for content, looked up at me and said, "You and every other woman in town."

"No, you don't understand. I have some evidence— actually it's a feeling, but it has to do with the Portello case. Just give him the note. He'll know what to do."

"Sure, no problem," she laughed. "What case did you say that was?"

"Portello."

"Never heard of it."

Red-faced and furious, I blindly rushed out of the one-story building, and ran smack into a tall uniform worn by Sergeant Fishburn. I jumped back and apologized while the officer grinned, and grabbed my shoulders, probably fearing I was going to tip over on the uneven cobblestones.

"Looking for someone, Ms Stuart?"

"Sergeant, just the person I need to talk to," I gulped and smoothed my hair down.

"I'm off duty. Would you like to go for a cup of coffee?"

"Well, yeah … I mean, sure, but you're off duty…."

"The case we're going to talk about is officially unofficial," he grinned. He walked me down the sidewalk to a bakery/coffee shop and scored a table in the far corner. The place smelled like heaven and hummed with noisy chatter from its many customers.

I sat across from Fishburn's intense blue eyes, trying to remember why I wanted to talk to him. I noticed for the tenth time there was no ring on his left ring finger. He saw my glance and focused on my naked ring finger. Our server arrived with two cups of coffee. Unfortunately, the chatty waitress felt the need to drop by and ask if everything was all right every five minutes.

"So what's this 'unofficial case' about?"

"The department doesn't have time to look into

something that was written up as an accident. That was my fault. I should have listened to you. I became curious and checked into this black Nissan we found at the bottom of a cliff. Seems it was rented and went off the cliff the same day Mr. Portello was run over. I don't believe in coincidences."

"I don't either." I suddenly forgot the blue eyes and remembered everything I had wanted to tell the Sergeant. As I spoke, he jotted notes in his little book. When I finished, he slipped the book into his shirt pocket and took a last gulp from his coffee mug.

"Josephine, would you like to continue this conversation over dinner some time?"

Blindsided and blushing, I said, "Actually I have this boyfriend, I mean, I had this … it's still a little early … you know what I mean? But thank you for working on the case."

"I understand, Josephine. Give me your number and I'll be in touch."

I gave him my phone number and we went our separate ways. My way was the highway to Watsonville and my favorite market. I sat in the parking lot remembering the conversation with Fishburn, cheeks flushed, heart racing. Maybe there was "life" after David, but I still could not imagine being without him.

CHAPTER SIXTEEN

If Bratworse and Solow had not conspired to wake me, I would have slept through half of Friday, enjoying my dreams. Sir David and Sir Fishburn were jousting for the love of their fair lady who happened to be me until this blond in a red dress rode up on her pink Mustang. Everybody knows it's hard to compete with a Mustang.

I ignored the bad ending to my dream and rolled out of bed. By nine o'clock, the sun had found its way through dissipating morning fog. I finished my chores and checked a week's worth of emails. I found one from David. My heart raced. What if it was mean spirited? I opened it. He wrote that he was visiting his son in Modesto for a few days. He said he was sorry to be so busy. His niece was in town and needed a ride up to Modesto because Harley had hired her to be Monica's nanny for the summer.

I thought about the email all the way into Santa Cruz, wondering if the young woman I saw in David's car was his niece. He could have called me … actually he did. He left a message but the brat broke my answering machine. Maybe it was time to turn in my retro-message machine and my dumb phone for a smart phone, or turn in my cat for a teddy bear.

I parked in the lot behind the rink and tried to sort out my feelings. David had written about going to Modesto as if nothing had happened between us. Was he so callous that he mentioned nothing about our relationship … or lack of? Was there still hope that we would reconcile our differences? I climbed out of the truck in deep thought.

Bonnie walked up to my window. "Hey, Josephine, I got a lady over here who wants to talk to you." Smoke poured from her mouth and nose.

"Myrtle?"

"Yeah, she said the rink was locked up tight. I told her to stick around."

"Thanks; I'll be over there in a minute. I just want to put these bags inside." I unlocked the door and left my two heavy canvas bags full of painting supplies near the front counter. From there, I walked over to Bonnie's place and found four senior women in a lively game of poker. Myrtle wore a red polyester pantsuit and black socks—no shoes. There were four piles of chips in the middle of the table along with a fake diamond tennis bracelet, dime store pearl earrings, a bottle of Rolaids and a pair of red Keds.

I stepped back and waited for the next hand to be played.

At the end of the round, Myrtle had her shoes back plus a bracelet and earrings. She told one wrinkly white-haired woman to keep her Rolaids.

Bonnie reminded the ladies that strip poker was not allowed. I was sure she said it more for my benefit than theirs.

"Josephine, I've been looking all over for you," Myrtle said, as I bent down and gave her a hug. She turned back to her friends. "Don't anybody touch my stack of chips while I'm gone."

"So I guess you're going with me?"

She nodded, pulled on her red Keds, latched a hand onto my elbow and trundled over to the back entrance of the rink. We entered, and I pointed out the words from the Hokey Pokey song painted across the wall. She commented on the clouds and birds and finally the half-finished faux counter.

I offered Myrtle a seat on a bench. She plopped down like whipped cream on a hot sundae.

"Are you OK, Myrtle?"

"Certainly, just need a moment to catch my breath. Remember when I told you about those dead dogs? The whole neighborhood was upset about the barking. Nicki blamed Mario because she never liked him, but it could have been anyone with a little poison and a chunk of hamburger."

"Did she do anything about it? Call the police? Anything?"

"She had the police over there, but so far they haven't come up with any evidence. Too many murder and robbery cases to solve—they say." Myrtle rolled her eyes, adding to the clownish look her off-kilter wig gave her.

"Did you know that Gianna hangs around with Nicki?" I asked.

Myrtle nodded. "I guess Nicki doesn't hold anything against Gianna that Mario did. All I know is that she comes down to Bonnie's Bingo Parlor every Saturday night with Tammy, my niece. They like to play a couple hours of bingo before the roller derby starts. Nicki and Bonnie are old friends. The three of them used to be on a team together.

"So they were roller derby girls?"

"Yep. You can take me back to Bonnie's now," she said, giving me both hands so I could pull her up from the bench. "You know, I feel sorry for Nicki. No wonder she likes to get out of the house, away from a cranky old husband and a rotten son who should have moved out years ago." Myrtle shuffled toward the back exit, one hand gripping my elbow.

"I have some news on the case. Turns out Mario was run over by a rented car."

"You're kidding!" Myrtle turned to look at me.

"How do you know that?" she asked, as we entered Bonnie's place.

"Sergeant Fishburn is on the case, and he told me they found a black Nissan at the bottom of a cliff in Monterey County, rented the same day as the murder."

"A black Nissan? What about it?" Bonnie asked as she escorted us to the poker table.

"A black rental car was found on the beach. The Sergeant thinks it's the one that ran over Mario." I stepped back from the table, saying I had to get back to work, and darted out the door before Bonnie could get any more information out of me.

The rink smelled of new and old timbers and something sweet and spicy. I figured it was a combination of smells from the new construction plus the new carpet in the office. I settled down to my work, creating irregularities and highlights in the faux redwood boards around the base of the counter. As I worked, the Hokey Pokey song ran through my head like a catchy TV commercial. "You put your right foot in, you put your right foot out, you put your right foot in and you shake it all about," I sang to myself.

After four hours of painting and Hokey Pokey nonsense, I stood back to catch the full effect of my brushwork. It still needed a couple of clear coats, but the sides of the counter looked like they were made out of redwood. I smiled and my stomach growled.

I checked my watch. It was almost two o'clock, and I was hungry enough to eat dirt. I locked up the rink and headed over to Charlie Hong Kong's. As I passed by the barbershop, I peeked in the large front window. All the lights were off and a sign hung on the door that read, "Gone Fishing." I smiled. Grady was a private man. He probably didn't want to share his heartache. This was his way of keeping things light.

Normal lunch hours were over. More people were

leaving the noodle place than where arriving. I had my choice of places to sit. One smiley customer waved me over to his table.

"Chester, what brings you back to the old neighborhood?"

"I just started a remodel a couple blocks from here. How's your work coming along?"

"I'm just about finished with the marble and redwood. Excuse me, Chester, while I order my lunch." I walked over to the guy behind the counter and ordered. Chester and I chatted, my food arrived and my favorite carpenter said he would drop by sometime to see the fauxed counter. He said his new client might be interested in having some faux work done at the remodel.

After lunch, I walked back to the rink, locked the main entrance doors, packed up my painting equipment and lugged it out to the truck. The Hokey Pokey song still played in my head like a bad record on steroids. I dropped my purse in the front seat and stowed the canvas bag under the dash. I couldn't remember if I had locked the front door to the rink, so I locked my truck, dropped the keys in my pocket and went back into the building. A rush of skater-kids would arrive in ten minutes, but I checked the front doors just to be safe.

I peeked into the new office and noticed that the little throw rug was rolled to one side of the room and the trapdoor was ajar. I started to straighten it, but decided to go down and take another look at the safe. Grady once told us we had a one-in-64,000 chance of coming up with a correct three-digit combination. Fat Chance!

I set the little trapdoor aside and zipped down the rabbit hole. I turned on the lights as musty air with a hint of something sweet and spicy filled my nostrils. It was the first indication that someone had been in the tunnel recently.

First, I checked the desk to see if the pictures were still there, wishing I had counted them so I would know if any were missing. The drawer was open and all the photos were missing. I figured Ralph was too big to enter the downstairs tunnel, but Ashley could easily haul her little designer jeans up and down the ladder. Who else would go down the rabbit hole? I was the only worker left on the job, so who took the pictures and why?

Suddenly I heard people running across the floor above me, children laughing and skates grinding across the wood floor. But the worst sound was the trapdoor falling into place.

I scampered up the ladder and pushed against the door. It wouldn't budge. I yelled for someone to let me out, but the clatter and chatter of humanity was much louder than my futile cries for help. The throbbing noise increased as the rink filled with skaters, finally leveling off at a loud roar. My voice was no match for squealing children, stomping skates and music from the loudspeakers.

I made my way down the ladder with no more fight and no more voice, feeling defeated. I went to the little room with the desk, settled into the one and only chair and prepared myself for nine hours of waiting for closing time at midnight. By that time, the rink would quiet down and someone might hear my calls for help. As if I weren't depressed enough, the stupid Hokey Pokey song ran non-stop through my tired brain for the next eight hours. Finally around eleven, I let my chin rest on my chest and closed my eyes.

Even sleep could not rescue me from the Hokey Pokey. I dreamed I was looking at Hokey Pokey graffiti scrawled across a long concrete wall inside the police station. Most of the words had black letters, but the word *you* was always painted in red. I asked Kyle why he painted all the *you*'s with red paint. He denied having done such a thing, and pointed to a shadowy figure across the room. The shadow dissolved into a dark corner, but I felt I knew the shadow by his small stature.

I woke up feeling cold with a full-body kink and drool on my cheek. I pulled my head up from the desktop, wiped my face with my sleeve and shivered. Cotton shirt, jeans and flip flops were not enough to keep a person warm when trapped underground ... trapped under ground! The worst part hit me when I realized the noise was gone. No grinding, stomping skates, and no shrieks of laughter from the skaters. Even the music had stopped.

I blinked my sleepy eyes, and checked my watch. It was two in the morning. The building was quiet because it was empty, except for one silly intruder in the basement. Maybe someone would see my truck and come looking for me. But no one came. The rink stayed quiet as time moved slowly forward. The complete quiet irritated me at first.

The spooky dream about graffiti at the police department played in my head while my stomach grumbled. I ignored my empty stomach, closed my eyes and visualized the Hokey Pokey words, all black except for the word *you* which was always red. Each four-line stanza had four red *you*'s. Each three-line stanza had two red *you*'s. Between the four-liners were the three-liners.

The Hokey Pokey was all about a right foot, left foot, right arm, left arm—like the dial on a combination lock—right, left, right, left. What if the number of *you*'s mattered?

You put your right foot in—you turn the combination lock to the right, then left, then right and so on. I decided to fiddle with the lock. It was obviously a functional antique. At least it would give me something to do, and what if the first number really was the number of *you*'s in the first stanza?

I took a deep breath and moved closer to the cast iron door, gripped the center of the large numbered dial, twirled it to the right and then to the left, slowly bringing the arrow to zero.

In the noiseless underground cavern, I asked for guidance, held my breath and calmly turned the dial to the number four notch. In the absolute quiet of two o'clock in the morning, I heard a faint click and froze. Did the click mean that my first guess was correct? Heart pounding, I moved the dial carefully to the left and stopped at the number two notch. Again I heard a faint click, despite my booming heartbeat.

My hands felt clammy. I rubbed them up and down my jeans a couple of times, sucked in some stale air, blew it all out and turned the dial slowly to the right. The click happened when the arrow hit the number four notch. I wiped my brow with one hand and pulled on the handle of the safe with the other but nothing happened. Obviously I needed another number so I used number two from the fourth pokey stanza.

I heard the click! But the door wouldn't open.

"Dang! What's with this stupid door?" I straightened up, stomped three steps to the ladder and three steps back. I wiped my sweaty hands, gripped the steel handle with both hands, and pulled back hard.

"Oh my God!" I blinked and looked again. "How can this be?"

CHAPTER SEVENTEEN

Dumbfounded, I stared into a black abyss. The air was anything but fresh. I pulled my head back from the opening and closed the safe door halfway. Despite the stale air, my curiosity forced me to re-open the door. I flipped a light switch. Nothing had prepared me for what I saw as two rows of florescent lights blinked on. Instead of looking into a safe, I was stepping into a brightly lit room the size of a small bedroom.

An old wooden easel stood in one corner beside a cardboard box with about twenty canvases lined up and poking out the open top. Against one wall was a cot with a grey wool blanket folded neatly at one end. A stool and a three-drawer cabinet sat on a dusty braided rug and a very retro refrigerator monopolized another corner. I heard the soft purring of its motor. The fridge and all the furniture must have been installed before the tunnel was completed, before there was a little trap door to keep people out and furniture in.

I thought back to the first time I met Tom Trippy and tried to remember the stories he told us. He had mentioned something about a tunnel, a metal door and furniture.

I discovered oil painting supplies in the little cabinet. The paint tubes looked old and some were dried up, but Mario had taken excellent care of his brushes. A can of paint thinner and a stack of rags filled the second drawer. The bottom drawer held camera equipment; an old single-lens reflex Nikon camera neatly stored in its case, several rolls of film and three bottles of chemicals. Chemicals for what?

I looked around the room. Next to the easel, behind the cardboard box was a small door about five feet tall. I pushed the box of canvases aside and turned the doorknob. The door squeaked open. I felt a string dangling from the ceiling and pulled on it. A red light bulb turned everything in the little closet-room red, the counter top, the metal trays and a rope that stretched across the room with clothespins to hold wet photographs. Mario had created his own little world with everything he needed.

My stomach growled. My mouth was parched. I pulled the light string and shut the door. The bright lights in the main room seemed to be more welcoming. I pushed the box back in front of the door where I found it, not that Mario would care. I pulled a canvas from the box and held it up. The picture was of a pre-teen redheaded girl concentrating on buttoning the waistband of her plaid skirt. Her curly pigtails were backlit by light from a window. A pair of skates sat on the bench beside her. It was signed, MP.

The canvases were of uniform size. My guess was sixteen by twenty inches, a popular size for portraits. I examined painting after painting in complete awe over the use of light, the loose style, soft colors, deep shadows and amazing textures the artist had rendered. Each oil painting told a story. The subjects were all ages and descriptions doing what young girls do. They were caught brushing their hair, chatting, dressing, stretching, lounging and daydreaming. The style was a mixture of Renoir, Rembrandt and Degas.

The initials, MP, had to be Mario Portello's, since it was his tunnel and his safe. Putting the peephole, the photos and the paint supplies together was easy, but why had the poor man hidden his talent under a bushel?

I inspected and admired each painting a second time, dropping them gently one by one back into the box. I had come across one more reason to care about Mario, feeling that I knew him by his art. He was shy and sensitive, which in my mind balanced whatever he had done to cause his murder. Mario's paintings would stay in my mind for the rest of my life, like Michelangelo's "The Creation of Adam," and Van Gogh's "Starry Night." When something is really good, you never forget it. It would be like trying to forget David.

Naturally my thoughts went to David. He would have put a damper on the tunnel operation if he had known about it. I felt sure Mom would have sided with him along with Alicia. I never could understand how most people didn't get excited about curious events. They didn't question the odd glimpse of someone running down the sidewalk or climbing a fence. I tended to treat occurrences like that as suspicious. A guy running down the street with a pack on his back could have just robbed a bank, and the guy scaling the fence might be running from the law. Or maybe I watched too much television.

David would be out-of-his-mind worried about me if he knew I was missing. Did anyone know I was missing? Maybe Alicia wondered why I didn't go to her house for dinner Friday night. Did she try to call me? My cell phone was neatly stashed in my purse on the driver's seat of my truck. Would Bonnie go for a smoke and wonder why my truck was still there? Would she look inside and see my purse?

Out of habit, I checked my watch. It was four in the morning, three more hours until breakfast time. My stomach growled again. And then it occurred to me that Mario might have kept refreshments in the fridge. Maybe some sodas or....

I pulled hard on the refrigerator door. It seemed to be stuck—frozen over actually. I finally managed to get the door open but immediately slammed it shut. My body shook as I questioned my eyesight and my sanity. Did I really see what I thought I saw?

I sat down on the stool and tried to recover my wits. But the only thing left to do was take another look to see if I was hallucinating or not. I took a deep breath and pulled the door open. *Oh my God!* I did see what I thought I saw. The inside of the fridge had been stripped of its innards and a fully clothed body was bent like a pretzel and stuffed into the space. One frosty hand held a gun. I slammed the door shut.

My heart raced and my legs felt weak. I stretched out on the cot and pulled the itchy blanket over my body and my head. I squeezed my eyes closed and sang the Hokey Pokey song, but the dead man's image was still in front of my eyes. I understood why Mario left the gun in the man's hand. It was because Mario was innocent. John Doe had brought the gun to Mario. I imagined Mario struggling with the fellow and the gun going off accidentally. I had no ideas on where the struggle had taken place.

I wrapped the blanket around my shoulders and paced. I stepped into the tunnel and walked eight steps from the ladder to the end of the hall, and eight steps back. I climbed the ladder over and over, hoping that exercise would warm up my legs. In spite of my hopes, time stood still and my feet were freezing.

When I ran out of things to do, I pulled out the oil paintings and admired them all over again. Why were the paintings stuffed away where no one could appreciate them?

I closed the safe door and entered the little office, telling myself not to think about the body in the next room. I remembered what Ralph had said about Mario's reaction to the plans for a mural. Mario must have had a big laugh over that. His secret combination in big letters for everyone to see, but no one would realize what they were looking at.

Out of boredom, I checked the desk drawer for secret compartments and such. I ran my hand up behind the drawer and then pulled the drawer out and set it on top of the desk. It was just a drawer—until I turned it upside down. A large envelope was taped to the bottom board. The paper envelope looked old and fragile. The flap was not sealed, just tucked in. I carefully opened the flap and peered inside.

Gingerly, I pulled out a five by seven black and white photograph of a little girl looking into the camera with a happy smile on her perfect little face. I turned the picture over and read two lines of longhand. "Mary Rose Portello, three years old. Our very own blessed angel on earth."

There was one other item in the envelope, an article cut out of a newspaper. Somehow I knew what it would be. A knot was growing in my dry throat, and tears ran down my cheeks when I read the first sentence. Mary Rose Portello choked on a pear and died at the tender age of three years old.

We have all heard of cases where a child dies and so does the marriage. I finally understood Gianna's heartache, and Mario's reclusive life-style. If only they had been able to talk about it. Surely someone could have helped them. I slipped the picture and article back in the envelope, dropped it in the drawer and maneuvered the drawer into its proper place.

Feeling cold and alone, I laid my head down on the desktop for a little rest.

The next time I looked at my watch, it was nine o'clock in the morning. My neck felt like it was stuck in a permanent tilt to the right, and my tongue was stuck to the top of my mouth—dry as sawdust. An uncomfortable sadness hung over me like the prickly blanket around my shoulders.

Once my mind began to function, I formed a plan of action. I collected up two of the metal trays from the dark room, walked over to the ladder and set them down. When the rink opened for business at noon, I would smash the trays together over and over until someone heard me. I decided to try them out first so I would know how hard I had to slam them together. Like two square symbols, I crashed them into each other with all my might.

The noise was substantial. I hoped it would be enough.

I heard something and looked up to the top of the ladder. Someone was in the building.

The trapdoor opened. I saw a pair of men's shoes.

CHAPTER EIGHTEEN

The shoes were a blur through my tears of joy. As the trapdoor was kicked aside, I saw the lower half of a pair of Levis, then a white smock, the blue collar of a button down shirt, and then I sneezed.

"Bless you," came a man's voice as he bent down to see me better. "Josephine, what are you doing down there?"

"I'm coming up—thank God you're here!" A surge of hope and energy pushed me forward, up the ladder until it occurred to me that Grady was in the building alone. How did he get in and why was he there? I stopped mid-rung.

"Need help?" he asked.

"No, no, I'm fine." The blanket slipped off my shoulders and fell to the concrete floor as I climbed out of the rabbit hole with Grady holding my arm. He led me over to a bench. I willed myself not to sit down. What if I needed to run? "Grady, I don't want to seem snoopy ... but, ah, why are you here ... alone?" I shivered.

Grady put an arm over my shoulder. There would be no way for me to run.

"I had a client cancellation so I decided to work on the safe. Ralph gave me a key to the front door and told me about the trapdoor key in the candy jar. He said I could work on the safe any time."

"Well, you won't need to bother with it. I figured out the combination and opened the safe because the Hokey Pokey song kept running through my head, you know, like a catchy commercial." I finally sat down on the cold bench.

Grady sat down beside me and draped his barber coat over my shivering shoulders. He listened intently to every word I said, my whole crazy story about what had happened in the last twenty hours. His face reflected shock, worry and pain as if he were experiencing first-hand my traumatic misadventure. His eyes widened and his jaw dropped when I told him about the body. He said he would call the police.

I rattled off Fishburn's number. Why had I bothered to memorize it?

Grady made the call and fed me candy and peanuts from the vending machine until Sergeant Fishburn arrived, then apologized to the two of us for having to hurry back to his barbershop.

Fishburn and I sat on the bench, our upper bodies turned toward each other, knees touching. He searched my face as if it would give him the story without my having to come up with the words. Since I had just told Grady everything, the whole ugly tale poured out of my mouth effortlessly, like flushing a toilet to make room for clean water. The biggest relief happened when I told Fishburn about the body.

"Thank you, Ms. Stuart, for your detailed account. Please excuse me while I make a few calls."

While the Sergeant used his phone, I walked on shaky legs to the water fountain for a drink. I felt permanently parched after twenty hours of no liquids. If the water had germs, they tasted great. As I let another gulp trickle down my throat, I saw movement near the main entrance and cranked my head around to see who was entering the building.

The door closed and Chester walked toward me.

In his easy manner, Chester asked me to name the faux finishes so that he could talk to his client about them. His calm demeanor told me he didn't know anything about my underground stay. I wiped water from my chin and began telling him about my terrible ordeal.

Chester's chin dropped. He put a hand up. "Wait a minute, Josephine, are you saying you were locked in the tunnel overnight?"

"That's what I'm saying. Someone had been in the tunnel so I went down to check on things."

"You're not going to like this. I told Ralph I was coming over here to meet with you. He asked me to go down and get the photographs for him. The place wasn't locked, but you weren't around so I got the photos and left. But later, I remembered I had left the trapdoor open. The front door was locked so I waited a few minutes until three o'clock when the rink opened, went inside, put the top on the rabbit hole, and locked it. You're not laughing, Jo."

"Maybe it will hit my funny-bone later, when I'm not so tired and freaked out."

"Sorry, Josephine. I had no idea you were down there."

I had a sudden urge to talk to David, even if he didn't want to talk to me. I was ready to risk making a fool of myself over the man who was constantly on my mind. I asked Chester if I could borrow his phone. He handed it to me looking like it was the least he could do.

Fishburn called the coroner, investigators and the crime scene cops while I called David's number. After five rings, I was ready to hang up.

"Hello, David. I thought you would never answer."

"Hi, Josie; I was making a sandwich for lunch. I just got back from Modesto last night and I called you this morning but you were already gone...."

"Actually, I was gone all night."

"Sweetie, I've been thinking. I tried putting myself

in your place, like what if I liked mysteries the way you do, and my friends and family didn't take me seriously. I guess I know how you feel now, and I'm so sorry for not understanding. I still don't like you getting into dangerous situations, but I'll stay out of your way. I have no right to interfere. Did you say you were gone all night?"

"I was accidentally locked in the tunnel I told you about." My throat felt like chalk dust as my voice faded to a low rasp.

"I think we have a bad connection. At least you called me and I know you're fine. How about dinner tonight at the Grill?"

"Sure," I smiled, and signed off. I should have called Mom and Dad, but if they didn't know I was missing, why call and upset them. But I did call Alicia. In my withering voice, I asked her to take me home. She didn't ask questions, just listened to my pitiful ramblings, and promised to come and get me right away.

Worry lines appeared on Fishburn's forehead as he told me not to leave town because he wanted to talk about the case in a day or two, when I felt up to it.

An investigator had strung yellow tape around the trapdoor by the time the Quintanas arrived. Trigger was wide-eyed curious, especially about the lumpy body bag lying on the floor near the restrooms. Ernie quickly took the boy's hand and led him to the backdoor.

Alicia and I followed the boys to the parking lot.

Ernie drove Trigger in my truck, and I rode with Alicia in her Volvo. At her request, I told my story one more time as we headed toward the comfort of home.

As we motored up Otis, I automatically looked up David's driveway. Our eyes met as he drove his car down to the road. Alicia slowed the car; I waved; David waved and the Volvo continued another hundred yards to my driveway. I cranked my head around and watched David make a sharp right turn and head toward town. I was sure he had no idea how badly I needed one of his comforting bear hugs. On second thought, I would have a bath and pull myself together before I saw him again.

The Quintanas dropped me at my house, making me promise to get some rest and call them if I needed anything. They were such a comfort.

Solow and Bratworse greeted me with howls, yowls, and huge appetites. I fed them first, knowing they had been outside all night and had missed a couple meals. Without further ado, I put myself to bed, falling asleep the moment I hit the sheets.

***

"Rap, rap, rap," cut into my dreams. I finally realized someone was pounding on my front door. Was it time to go to dinner with David? I checked the clock radio. Four o'clock. I stood up, straightened my shirt and ran fingers through my hair.

Solow barked at the door, a husky bark reserved for people he didn't know.

"Who's there?"

"Gianna Portello."

I opened the door and welcomed the pale, trembling widow into my house. I pointed to the sofa and she plopped down. I sat in the rocker wondering how the woman could look so different, so disorganized, definitely unglued.

"Josephine, dear, you must have endured a lot in that terrible tunnel. Sergeant Fishburn called me an hour ago and told me what happened to you. He said he will be asking me questions tomorrow at the police station." Gianna sniffed and wiped away a tear. "I called Alicia and she thought I ought to talk to you."

"No problem, Gianna. I'm glad you're here."

"My problem is," Gianna sniffled, "I had made it a habit to stay out of Mario's business. He lived his life and I lived mine. It was our way of dealing with the terrible loss of our daughter. Now I wish I had been there for him. How can I defend him against a murder charge when I don't know anything about his life?"

"Are they saying Mario murdered the man I found in the tunnel?" I asked, feeling like it was a real possibility.

"Sergeant Fishburn said my husband is a person of interest, and we all know what that means," she sniffed. "I can't imagine Mario hurting anyone, ever."

"Gianna, I've been studying the situation for weeks. If Mario killed someone, it must have been in self-defense. I studied his paintings. They were sweet, gentle, and beautiful—not something a murderer could create. I think he was a gentle man, defending himself, not a killer."

"Josephine, I know I have been acting disinterested up until now, but believe me, I truly want to know who ran over my husband." Her cheeks reddened as she swiped at a tear.

I rocked my chair back and forth. "I've put together a few facts and my own list of 'persons of interest.' Your husband's killer drove a rented black Nissan sedan, and later ditched it over a cliff. Ralph and his wife have been lying about their time spent in Hawaii and several of Mario's renters were very upset with him, afraid he would go through with his plan to raise the rent. Even your friend, Nicki, was mad at him."

"Josephine, thank you for sharing this information with me. Sadly, I have finally realized how many years I wasted, always thinking Mario and I would resolve our differences someday. Now it's too late. But I want to clear Mario's name and find his killer."

"If you think of anything that will help, please let me know, Gianna. We'll work on this together. As far as your interview with the police, just be honest. Tell them as much as you know. Can I get you a cup of tea?"

"Tea would be lovely." She wrapped her arms around her waist as if it were a cold day. "In the beginning, we were a good couple, Mario and I ...."

I decided to go to the kitchen and put the teakettle on, giving Gianna a little time to pull herself together. As soon as I turned my back, she screamed.

I twirled around and swatted Brat off her shoulder. The little monster had leaped from his favorite spot on the windowsill behind the sofa, and dug his claws into her white silk blouse, raking the material to shreds.

"I'm so sorry, Gianna. Let's sit in the kitchen and I'll put the little monster outside."

"Oh, don't do that. I'll calm him down." She reached down, picked up Bratworse and cuddled him in her hands until he fell asleep. I made a mental note to try her technique sometime.

We moved into the kitchen and I put the kettle on the stove. I asked her about each person on my list of suspects. She thought Mario's sister, Celeste, had the temperament for murder and she didn't trust Mr. Bauer's wife as far as she could throw her. But she could offer no strong motive for murder. When I told her about the paintings in the tunnel, she admitted she didn't know that Mario had painted anything else after he finished a portrait of her and then their daughter decades ago.

After Gianna left, I had an hour before David arrived. I showered and dressed for a night on the town, never mind that there was only one place to go in Aromas. The Grill was noisy with music and the chatter of friendly customers. We leaned closer to hear each other. The closer we were, the closer we wanted to be.

It was a starry night of loving bliss.

CHAPTER NINETEEN

Sunday morning seemed like a dream. I rested my head on the pillow for a while with my eyes closed, asking myself if David and I were really back together. Did he really listen to my "trapped in the tunnel" story and not accuse me of being a thoughtless snoop? Did he really wish me luck at solving the case? I thought about our date from start to finish. It was all true. David seemed to understand why I needed to solve the murder, comparing me to people who are hooked on solving crossword puzzles. I let his remark slide.

It was a night to remember. We had just finished our fabulous salmon and pasta entrée and drained our wine glasses. I thought the romantic dinner at the Grill was coming to an end, and then the Trippys arrived. Tom pulled a chair out for Lois. She giggled, sat down and they quickly became part of our dining experience. She talked excitedly about a recent shopping trip in San Francisco where they had stayed three nights at the Fairmont Hotel.

From there, Tom talked about another little get-away they were planning—three days at their cabin in Boulder Creek. They would drive to the San Lorenzo Valley on Tuesday, outsmarting the holiday rush of Memorial Day vacationers. Tom turned to David and asked if we would like to join them for a few days.

All I could think of were the police and coroner's reports due next week. I wanted to know who the murdered person was and how he died as soon as possible, hopefully before the newspapers got hold of it. I believed the information would lead to Mario's murderer.

I only half-listened to Tom's yammering about fishing, hiking and great dining in Boulder Creek. But I paid more attention when he repeated the invitation of three days in the forest.

David looked hopeful as he turned his eyes to me. "I'm not busy Tuesday…." he said.

"I, ah … don't think … I, ah…."

"Wonderful, dear, we'll have a great time together," Lois giggled, and took another sip of wine. "We can play cards, horseshoes, swim…."

"Thank you, Lois. I'm sure it will be fun." Images of a dip in the icy stream, wild animals, poison oak and a lumpy bed instantly came to mind. "What shall I bring?"

"Don't worry about a thing, dear; we generally eat out."

For me, that statement punched a hole in the only good parts of being in the great outdoors—campfires, the smell of sizzling bacon, hotdogs on a stick, fresh trout and burnt marshmallows. But after a deep breath and a moment's thought, I decided a vacation in the redwoods might be just what I needed, a way to relax and enjoy David's new attitude.

"You'll bring that crazy dog of yours, won't you?" Tom asked me.

"He comes with a kitten."

"A kitten! How sweet," Lois purred.

Some kittens might be sweet but not mine. But I still had hopes for a miracle.

I blinked my eyes open, stretched and looked around my bedroom for Solow, leaving the rest of my date with David for future daydreams. I found Solow and Bratworse sitting by the back door. I let them out and shuffled back down the hall to the bathroom for a shower. My daydreaming continued as I lathered and rinsed everything, head to toe. Still wearing a smile, I toweled off, pulled on my robe and sashayed into the kitchen where I instructed Mr. Coffee in the art of coffee making.

The phone rang. I answered.

It was Alicia. After ten minutes of reassuring her that I was fine, she asked me to go with her to the big roller derby Memorial Day celebration at the rink. Her neighbor had extra tickets because his daughter, Kati, skated for the Santa Cruz team and he had been roped into singing the *Star Spangled Banner* at the event.

I hadn't done well at the last derby, but Alicia needed a favor and I owed her quite a few so I said I would pick her up at seven-thirty.

I dashed out of the house at seven o'clock after a busy day of catch-up—catch-up on laundry, house cleaning, emails and rescuing Solow from Bratworse attacks, which were playful but tiring. I inhaled a protein drink as I fired up the Mazda and drove past David's house. Typically his Jeep sat in the garage and the Miata stayed in the driveway, ready for quick trips. The driveway was empty. I wondered where he was, but not in a negative way. Negative thinking was not allowed now that David and I were a couple again. I was determined to see only the best in his personality, expecting he would do the same for me.

I had barely stopped my pickup in front of Alicia's house when she stepped from the curb and climbed into the passenger seat. She wore white jeans, a jeweled cap and a big black purse with red pom poms peeking out the top. Obviously she was ready to cheer for Kati and the Boardwalk Bombshells against the Jet City Rollers. Their last confrontation had been a year ago and the score was 195 to 194. Santa Cruz would try to keep the lead.

Alicia filled me in on all the roller news, such as the

fact that the new Kaiser Arena on Front Street would be opening in three weeks, putting Ralph's place out of the roller derby picture. The new indoor rink/basketball court would seat a thousand people. Ralph's place could never compete with those numbers. Five rows of benches and two-hundred-square feet of standing room was all he had at the rink. But it would continue to be a great place for kids to skate and have their birthday parties and a place for the derby girls to practice.

We stood at the end of a double line of people half a block long, as a red sun hung low in the sky. I noticed a colorful South American cape worn by Gianna's neighbor, Nicki, about six people ahead of us.

"Jo, did you read *The Sentinel* this morning?" Alicia asked.

"No. I walked to the end of my driveway and looked everywhere. Guess it wasn't delivered. Why? Did I miss something?"

"Oh yeah! It seems that someone stole the body you found...."

"What? You have to be kidding!"

"I'm not kidding. I read that someone stole the body while everyone was gathering evidence inside the building. One officer was sitting in the driver's seat of the coroner's wagon eating his lunch when someone opened the back of the vehicle and swiped the body. Who would want a body?" Alicia grimaced. "They didn't even know it was missing until they got to the morgue."

"That body might be a clue in Mario's murder. I think the guilty person knows that and is hiding it." The line moved a few feet forward.

"Jo, did you know that you are a very suspicious person?"

"That's why I'm going to figure out who murdered Mario and why," I boasted, as I watched Nicki enter the building and six people later, it was our turn. Our tickets put us in the last row of benches, not exactly loge seats, but better than standing like the hundred people behind us. The noise level rose as the teams took turns warming up. Finally, a whistle blew and they wheeled themselves off the wood floor onto cement and stood with their backs against the rail.

Everyone stood up as Alicia's neighbor stepped out onto the rink and sang a fair rendition of the National Anthem accompanied by music from an overhead speaker while Kati held the flag. Nicki, Bonnie and Tammy, stood in front of us blocking our view.

Bonnie looked around. "Josephine, thought you didn't like this sort of thing?"

"Whatever gave you that idea?" I leaned forward. "Isn't that the health inspector next to Nicki?"

"Yeah, she finally got her old man out of the house," Bonnie said over the roar of spectators, as the two teams streamed onto the flat track. Five rows of people sat down, a whistle blew and the game started.

Alicia waved her hands and whistled. She frequently explained the action to me, but I never understood the scoring. The Boardwalk Bombshells were ahead by thirteen points. Their jammer had crashed through the Jet City's blockers over and over. Ten minutes later, we were ahead by fifty points. My job was to keep Alicia from hyperventilating, and her job was to keep me awake. I was suffering from the stuffy heat and bad air when the Jets made their move and scored eight points and then twelve more. The game tightened up to one 152 to 149. We were still ahead, barely.

Halftime didn't come a minute too soon. The whole roller rink population emptied out onto the front lawn quicker than you can say, ridiculous. Refreshments could be purchased from three charity food booths, the Girl Scout cookie booth, the Boy Scout popcorn booth and Avery's SPCA Shaved Ice. Since I was the first person out of the building and first in line for a snow cone, I had half the crowd pushing me from behind. I paid for my lemon and root beer ice with two spoons and inched myself sideways away from the booth.

I saw Alicia sitting in the grass near the sidewalk ten yards away. As I wove my way through the crowd, a woman dropped something in the grass and bent over to look for it. I felt a crunch under my right foot. She turned to look at me.

"Oh, Nicki, it's you. Remember me? I'm Gianna's friend…."

"I know who you are. Mind getting off my phone?" she snarled.

I wished I didn't have to raise my foot because I knew by the sound and feel of it, the stupid phone was in pieces. I moved my foot.

Nicki picked up the demolished phone the way one would pick up a dying baby bird. Her husband glared at me through his bifocals as if I had stepped on the phone purposely.

I apologized, backed up and squeezed through the crowd of 150 derby fans all milling around one petite patch of grass. I finally joined Alicia at the curb where we sat and ate the shaved ice, except for the yellow glop that had accidentally fallen on Jim Waller's shiny black shoe.

Deliciously flavored ice, twilight shadows and ocean breezes quickly gave us comfort, even a chill. A whistle blew, and we marched back into the stuffy building feeling refreshed and able to handle another round of noise and heat. The Bombshells held their lead and Santa Cruz fans went home happy.

Alicia thanked me for taking her to the derby. I dropped her at her house and drove on to Aromas. My brain told me to go home and get a good night's sleep.

But my heart told me to see if David was home. Typically my heart over-rides my brain.

David was home, he invited me in and we had a meaningful evening—more heart than brain. He told me he had been working all day on his plans for Boulder Creek. He showed me a tent he bought for the two of us in case the cabin was too crowded. He cleaned his garage looking for some old ropes and climbing equipment, and he cleaned the Jeep inside and out, reminding me of an excited little boy going on his first Boy Scout camping trip.

I remembered my first and last Girl Scout camping trip. We were in our sleeping bags trying to fall asleep to the sound of far away sirens. The stars were blocked out, the sky was red and we smelled smoke, but we were not evacuated. It had been a serious forest fire but not close enough for us to pick up and go. But children have big imaginations, so we worried and cried.

CHAPTER TWENTY

Monday started out like any normal weekday. Bratworse shredded my dining room drapes, fell into the toilet and swam a few laps before I found him, and after his bath, he toppled a jar of honey off the kitchen counter. I put the boys outside since the honey was mixed with broken glass. As I scraped honey off the floor, still day dreaming about my evening with David, the phone rang. I answered on the sixth ring, hands sticking to the phone.

"Josephine, I was beginning to think you weren't home ..."

"I'm home. Who is this?"

"Gianna. I have something to tell you ... it's rather urgent."

"Would you like to meet somewhere?" I asked.

"Yes, but not until tonight. I need you to come to my house at eleven o'clock. It's very important. Wear your old clothes and sneakers and bring your dog," Gianna's voice quivered.

"Ah, sure ... OK ..." The line went dead. My heart womped around in my chest telling me that something big was happening. If Gianna had wanted to scare me, she did a good job of it. Was this appointment something I should share with David? I thought it over and decided not to share since I had no clue what it was all about. Maybe it was just Gianna falling off the sanity boat.

My plan for Monday had been to go to the rink and add another round of clear coat to the fauxed counter sides and top, collect my money from Ralph and turn in my key. He had already paid for the mural; and I had spread the wealth to Alicia and Kyle, the grocery store, the mortgage company and so on. The next check would be mine to spend. Wildbrush Mural Company was in the black.

I called Ralph to make sure he would be at the rink, put a bowl of fresh water on the patio and left Solow and Bratworse outside. I told myself they would be just fine. They had five acres to explore; but knowing them, they would nap most of the day and create havoc half the night.

I motored through Aromas, hardly noticing the new Water District Building, the Dragonfly Gallery and the Post Office, let alone the neighborhoods and then the fields of lettuce and berries. It was all a familiar blur as my mind examined the murder suspects I had accumulated. I wondered for the hundredth time who had lived in the body I found. Who killed him and why? Who stole the body? It occurred to me that time was going by and our chances of finding the murderer were going with it.

I had so much to think about that I almost missed the Morrissey exit. A quick lane change, a couple indignant honks and I was off the freeway heading west on Soquel Avenue. I parked next to Myrtle's old white Caddie in the lot behind the rink and decided to poke my nose into Bonnie's place to see what Mom's neighbor was up to.

"Well, if it isn't Josephine. Looking for Myrtle?" Bonnie asked.

"Yeah, is she here?"

Bonnie nodded and pointed her thumb toward the back wall where four ladies were hunched forward concentrating on their cards. "She's hot. Better let her play."

Myrtle hadn't seen me and I didn't get a warm fuzzy

feeling of welcome from Bonnie, so I turned and carried my bag of paint supplies over to the back door of the rink. It wasn't locked. I walked in quietly and looked around. The banner advertising the big Memorial Day Meet was missing from the rafters. The place was clean and quiet except for a tapping sound coming from below, in the tunnel.

I shuddered but kept moving closer to the rabbit hole. The cover was off, so I quietly bent down to see who was there. I saw the top of a man's head, broad shoulders and a hammer in one hand.

"Rap, rap, rap." Someone pounded on the front entrance door. I stepped out of the office and walked to the door.

"Who's there?"

"Police."

I opened the door and let Sergeant Fishburn enter. He smiled when he saw me.

"Hi, Josephine. You look like you've recovered from your stay in the dungeon."

"Yes, I have. Any news on the body snatcher?"

"No, that's why I'm here. It's pretty embarrassing for the department, losing a body like that. I'm going to go over this place again for fingerprints. Ralph said he would meet me here."

"I just saw him in the tunnel. To tell you the truth, I thought he would be too big for the rabbit hole."

Several grunts came from the direction of the office.

Fishburn's eyes turned toward the new office, his brow furrowed.

I followed him inside the new little room. Two arms and the top of Ralph's hairy head protruded from the hole in the floor. The officer grabbed Ralph's arms and pulled, but the shoulders were stuck. I set my purse and paint bag on the floor, grabbed hold of Fishburn from behind and pulled. We made progress at first, until the man's belly became wedged.

Sweat ran down Ralph's forehead as he cursed under his breath.

I let go of Fishburn and he let go of Ralph. Ralph's eyes bulged as he forced his body back down into the hole and then breathed a loud sigh of relief. I shared an idea I had. What if Ralph backed down the ladder, wrapped himself with the masking tape I had in my bag of paint supplies, and one person pushed from behind while the other person pulled from the top?

The guys agreed that it might work. I was the designated taper/pusher. Ralph stepped away from the ladder as I descended. He had removed his shirt, revealing a large hairy belly. I used the whole role of masking tape, stretching it as tight as I could, marching round and round the well-fed gentleman who sucked his tummy in until his face turned red.

Ralph teetered up the ladder with me pushing his butt, scared to death he would fall backward and squish me on the floor below. Fishburn grabbed the extended arms and pulled while Ralph groaned and cursed. Eventually, we completed our task and my boss was free of the rabbit hole. If the tunnel hadn't been a crime scene, I think he would have sealed it up pronto and permanently.

I turned off the lights and scurried up the ladder, carrying Ralph's shirt.

Ralph's face was still red. He needed to breathe.

Fishburn worked at a piece of tape. "Josephine, you have fingernails...."

"OK, but don't blame me if it hurts," I warned Ralph, as I pulled a strip of tape free. The next piece was ripped directly from his hairy body. I learned one thing that day—grown men do cry. I'm sure those were tears running down his cheeks as I pulled round after round of tape from his plumpness. He didn't thank me for my efforts, but he didn't swat me either.

Fishburn and Ralph walked outside, probably for a little private talk, while I slathered clear coat on the sides and top of the fauxed counter with a three-inch brush. Half an hour passed. I cleaned my brush with water, packed up and left before the guys returned. It was better that way. I wasn't interested in Fishburn's flirtations, and Ralph could mail my paycheck.

Since it was almost noon, I decided to have lunch at Charlie Hong Kong's. I drove two blocks, parked the truck and entered the noodle shop five minutes before the lunch rush started. I ordered my chicken pesto noodles and sat down at a little table facing the front window where I entertained myself by watching cars go by. I saw Mr. Bauer enter Grady's barbershop a block and a half away. Kitty-corner from his shop was G's Boutique where Ashley Rattini was just leaving with two bags full. The woman must have had a closet the size of my living room.

Someone tapped me on the shoulder.

I whirled around to find Fishburn standing at my shoulder. He pulled up a chair.

"Have you ordered?" I asked.

"Nope. I saw your truck and decided to come in and see how you're doing. Things have changed for you, haven't they? I can tell by your eyes."

"What about my eyes?"

"They sparkle, even when you're taping up a guy's stomach."

"It turned out that my boyfriend didn't let me down. Everything is back to normal," I said, feeling my face flush. "Any news on the missing body?"

"Nothing has turned up yet. Nothing like this has ever happened in my career as a police officer. I still don't know how they did it and the coroner is going postal. He already fired the driver and his partner.

Apparently, the driver was talking on the phone—private call, and his partner was inside using the restroom."

"You used the word *they*? Do you mean there was more than one person stealing the body?"

He looked around the room. "I'm not supposed to say, but yeah, we have a witness who saw the whole thing from this window. He works here. Says it was an older couple driving a black SUV. That was all he could make out from here."

I looked down the street to see how well I could see things in front of the rink. I could make out the color and basic type of the vehicles parked at the curb, but that was all. The "older couple" description came from a young guy who had barely learned how to shave. The word *older* could mean my age and up. But the couple couldn't be too old and still lift the body. That narrowed it down to two people over fifty and under eighty, which was half the population of Santa Cruz.

Under Fishburn's gaze, I worked hard at looking casual while twirling and eating noodles without dropping them onto my favorite red t-shirt. I must have lost my concentration, because Mr. Blue Eyes reached over and plucked a noodle from my shirt. My face warmed up to the color of my shirt.

Fishburn excused himself, and I was left alone with half a bowl of noodles. From my nifty front window, I watched him drive away in the cruiser, wondering what it would be like to be the police officer who lost a body. I slurped noodles and counted in my mind couples that might have stolen the body. Did Gianna have a boyfriend? Did Bonnie or Celeste? Did Grady have a lady friend? What about the Bauers, Wallers and Rattinis? But the big question was why should I go to Gianna's house at eleven o'clock at night?

I would go because she sounded desperate.

I decided I needed a break from all the unanswered questions running through my mind. When the noodle bowl was empty, I fired up my truck and drove a couple miles to the west side of Santa Cruz where my parents lived. Walnut Street always gave me relief from the stress in my life. The tree-lined street, rows of Victorian-style homes, neat lawns and flower gardens soothed my senses. Mom and Dad's house was comparatively small and so was Myrtle's next door.

I curbed the pickup. One second later, something bumped my back bumper, and my head hit the horn. I rose up and looked into the rear view mirror. There was Myrtle climbing out of her old white Caddie. She hobbled along the sidewalk on bare feet.

I followed Myrtle up to her front door. She whirled around in slow motion when she heard me calling her name.

"Josephine, where did you come from?"

"Hi, Myrtle. I saw you drive up. Where are your shoes?"

"I lost my Keds to a pair of Kings," she grumped, and unlocked the front door. "Come in, Jo, and have a cup of tea. Did your Mom tell you they were going to Carmel for the day?"

CHAPTER TWENTY-ONE

I left Myrtle's house at two in the afternoon. She had a phone call while I was there, a call that took her into the den for almost fifteen minutes. I didn't know whether to finish my cup of tea and leave, or stay. She finally came back to the kitchen with new worry lines etched across her wrinkly forehead.

"Josephine, I'm sorry, but that was my niece. She was so upset. Her cat was run over last night about a block from her house. Hit-and-run."

"That's so sad. Isn't it funny, Myrtle, how everyone is sad when a pet dies, but when Mr. Potello was the victim of a hit-and-run, no one seemed to care?"

"Yes, yes, I see your point, dear." She added another scoop of sugar to her tea and tasted the lukewarm drink. "But that's not all...."

"Huh?"

"My niece also said her friend Bonnie was arrested for not cooperating with the police. She told Grady that she saw the body snatchers from her window, and he told the cops. She refuses to give a description to the police. My niece thinks Bonnie's protecting someone." Myrtle adjusted her wig. "Aiding and abetting if you ask me."

"Does that mean Bonnie's in the slammer?" I asked.

"Oh no, they questioned her at the police department and then drove her home. They warned her that she could get into big trouble if she knows who took the body," Myrtle explained.

"We can eliminate Grady and the Rattinis. But I still have five other suspects in mind."

"What kind of ghoul would steal a body?" Myrtle asked, wrinkling her nose.

"I have no idea, but I need to get on the road. Thanks for the tea, Myrtle. Call me if you hear anything else about the missing body." We hugged and I headed out the door.

Nine hours to go—nine hours of not knowing what in the world Gianna was up to. I needed to keep busy. I arrived home with a list in my head of things to do, like clean closets, water marigolds, train Bratworse to be a good kitten, give Solow a bath and call *The Sentinel* about the newspaper I didn't get. I wasn't avoiding David; I just wanted to remember my perfect date with him a little longer. Besides, I wanted to keep my rendezvous with Gianna a secret because he would definitely think it was strange and try to talk me out of it.

I decided to tackle Bratworse's training first. I had done a fair job training Solow when he was a pup. He knew how to sit, lie down, speak and sniff out anything alive or dead. I figured Brat was just a smaller version of my four-legged basset friend. It shouldn't be too difficult to civilize him.

Half a dozen scratch wounds later, Brat was faster than ever and I was pooped. The cat was like a wrecking ball and I had the house to prove it, what was left of it, so I turned my attention to Solow. He never liked his bath, but didn't put up a fuss. He tucked his tail tight under his belly as I soaked him with the hose, lathered him up and rinsed. In ten minutes, he went from smelling biodegradable earthy to smelling like tea tree and eucalyptus shampoo.

Feeling antsy, I took my boys for a walk up Otis Road, Solow on leash and Bratworse trailing behind. The Brat occasionally caught up to us and attacked Solow's back legs. Solow paid no attention. But when the brat attacked my bare ankle, I scooped him up and carried him the rest of the way home.

Solow loved to ride in my truck, but I hadn't taken him anywhere since Bratworse arrived. Without Solow's calming influence, the cat might hurt himself or raze my house to the foundation, so I decided to prepare a special "safe house" for the brat. I dusted off a wire bunny cage I had stored in the back yard. It had belonged to Thumper, who had gone to bunny heaven years ago. I checked it over for possible escape routes, and set the boxy cage on the washing machine, located on my back patio under a tin roof.

Once the Bratworse cage was stocked with water, milk and canned food, I began to prepare myself for an evening of "who knows what." I was told to wear old clothes. That would be easy because my closet was stuffed with old paint shirts and pants.

I washed down my eight o'clock dinner with iced tea, hoping I would be wide awake at eleven. Just thinking about it made me yawn. I poured a second iced tea, cleaned the kitchen and sat down on the sofa to watch a *Monk* re-run. The sit-com was so good I decided to watch another. I don't remember the second *Monk* show.

Sometime later, I opened my eyes and lifted my head off the back of the sofa. I looked around the living room feeling like I needed to remember something. My eyes focused on the clock next to the TV. It was ten-thirty.

"Ten-thirty!" I shouted as I stood up and looked around for Bratworse. After checking every room, I finally found the boys asleep on Solow's bed in my bedroom. I flipped the light on and they looked at me like, "Where's breakfast?"

"OK, Brat, you have to go to your new cage." I hustled him out to the starlit patio. He clung desperately to my t-shirt, sending sharp claws into my flesh. "There you go, Bratworse." I slammed the little door shut and hooked it.

Solow looked at me like I had just jailed his best friend. I hooked a leash to his collar, grabbed my purse and jacket and we ran to the truck. I hiked Solow into the passenger seat, ran around the cab, climbed into the driver's seat and turned the key. Minutes later, Aromas was behind us and the bright lights of Santa Cruz were half an hour away.

Traffic was light so I pushed the accelerator down hard, turned up the music and listened to Solow howl. He never complained about my singing and I didn't complain about his. It felt good having one-on-one time with my favorite guy and no Bratworse to mess it up. We made good time through Watsonville and Aptos. I checked my watch. We would only be a few minutes late, unless the red light coming up fast in my rearview mirror was the Highway Patrol.

I took my foot off the gas and pulled into the slow lane. I was preparing to pull over and stop when the Highway Patrol zoomed by and kept on going. I passed by the cruiser and its law-breaking SUV victim at the side of the road a couple miles down the highway. "If not for the grace of God...." I murmured, and kept my speed at the legal limit the rest of the way to Santa Cruz.

I left the freeway and drove west, through Santa Cruz to East Cliff Drive and Gianna's house. It was ten minutes after eleven and the neighborhood was ninety percent down for the night. Even Gianna's place looked dark. I parked at the curb and put my dog on leash. Less than a block away, a black sea lapped at the shore under a starry but moonless sky.

I plucked my little penlight from my purse and let Solow lead me up the walk to Gianna's front door. Had she forgotten I was coming? No porch light. I rang the bell.

Instantly, Gianna opened the door as if she had been watching for us. She ushered us in and closed the door gently. We stood in semi-darkness. The only light came from an inner hallway.

Solow gave the woman a little friendly woof.

She put her hands out and shushed him.

"What's the matter, Gianna?"

"We will have to be quiet, Josephine," she whispered. "I didn't want to tell you over the phone, but I witnessed something ... oh dear." She shivered and dropped into a chair.

"What is it, Gianna? We're here to help you."

"I'm glad you're here, but I don't know if I can go through with my plan."

"Tell me what it's all about and I'll help wherever I can," I said, as my legs trembled for a second. I folded into a chair next to Gianna who was holding her throat with both hands until she finally relaxed a bit.

"My neighbors, the Wallers, had ... have a son who lives in their basement. I haven't seen him in almost a month, not since around the time his dogs died. He thought Mario poisoned them...."

"But it was you," I said.

Gianna nodded. "I put poison in the ground beef and threw it over the fence. I couldn't stand those yappy monsters. They barked all day and half the night for months. They upset Mario too ... in fact, the whole neighborhood was ready to kill them and Animal Control wouldn't do anything except write citations. I thought I was doing everyone a favor. But the Wallers never got along with Mario and they blamed him right away. I should have confessed but I didn't. Even Mario didn't know I was the one who ... you know...."

"But that's not why I called you, Josephine. When I

came to your house Saturday, you asked me to keep you informed on anything new. At first, I wasn't going to tell you what I saw." She hesitated, as if she was having second thoughts about sharing what she knew.

"Gianna, I really appreciate your help. It seems like you and I are the only ones who want to know who the corpse is so that we can find Mario's murderer."

"You're right, so I'll tell you what I saw Saturday night from my bedroom window." She closed her eyes and took a deep breath. "It was two in the morning and I couldn't sleep. I heard noises, whispers outside, and a scraping sound. My window was already open. I peeked through the blinds and saw something moving next door. Nicki's side yard is easy to see into from my upstairs bedroom."

I held my breath.

Solow fell asleep at my feet.

"I kept listening and finally I realized what the scraping sound was. A shovel. Someone was shoveling in my neighbor's yard at two in the morning. I heard some sniffling and whispering. I saw two people— barely. One was shoveling and the other sat on something, head down, whimpering. I think that was Nicki, and I imagine Jim was shoveling. But I don't know anything for sure because it was a dark, foggy night. "

"What do you think they were digging?" I asked as my imagination ran to dead bodies, instead of petunias.

"When the hole was finished, they lifted something and put it in the hole. The big guy, who I am almost certain was Jim, filled the hole with dirt. Nicki had already left the scene. I think she went in the house. But the point is, I think the missing body is buried next door and it might be their son, Jimmy." Gianna's face paled to the color of milk.

"It certainly sounds like it. Maybe Jimmy was angry

about the dogs, went to the rink to kill Mario but the old man got the best of him somehow." My heart did a couple flip flops at the thought. If all this were true, it would point to Jim or Nicki as possibly being Mario's killer. Most likely Nicki since the witness said it was a woman driver.

"There's one problem…." Gianna sighed.

"Just one—I mean, what's the problem?"

"You probably know that Mr. Waller is running for Mayor of Santa Cruz."

I nodded.

"Well, I don't know how to say this, but Jim is well-connected. Nicki's my friend, but Jim scares me—always has. He gets what he wants and I think some of his friends are tough guys, if you know what I mean." She shivered. "Come upstairs with me and I'll show you the spot I'm talking about."

We tramped through Gianna's barely lit house, and felt our way up the stairs and into her bedroom. She walked over to a row of windows and held one of the blinds slightly open while I leaned close to the screened window. I stared into the black night until my eyes adjusted enough to make out a fence and sidewalk the length of the Waller's side yard, and a long swatch of ground between the fence and concrete. The fence separated Gianna's back yard from Nicki's side yard. Gianna's corner property faced East Cliff Drive and the ocean. Nicki's faced the side street, Martin Avenue.

"I see three garbage cans, a little shed and what looks like an over-turned boat of some sort. The only way we're going to know anything for sure is to go down there." I looked at Gianna.

"I agree. The Wallers usually go to bed around ten thirty—eleven. I don't see any lights over there so we could just go take a look, don't you think?"

"Why would we take a look instead of calling the

police?" I asked.

"Because Jim will kill me if he finds out I'm the one who called the police. He knows all the cops, and they would probably believe anything he tells them."

"What if there is a body over there? Do we dig it up and drop it off at the police department?" I joked.

"Josephine, what a great idea. That way no one knows who found it or how it got there. It would be identified and the ID would lead right to my neighbors." She made it sound so simple—so simple that goose bumps popped up all over my body.

CHAPTER TWENTY-TWO

Tuesday morning, David knocked on the front door at nine o'clock sharp. He had called at eight, wanting to get started on our Boulder Creek get-away, but I talked him down to nine o'clock at the earliest. After all, I didn't get home from Gianna's place until almost two A.M. that morning. Seven hours later, I was supposed to be packed and ready for a three-day trip to the Trippy cabin in the forest.

***

Of course, David didn't know about my late night activities and I wasn't about to tell him or anyone else. Body snatching wasn't something one bragged about. However, I was proud of Solow and the way he had led us straight to a section of dirt under a rowboat. Despite a noisy gate, awkward shovels, flashlights and a couple woofs from Solow, we made it to the Waller's side yard without incident. But that didn't stop my heart from racing at the thought of someone discovering us.

Unfortunately, an up-side-down ten-foot long rowboat covered the area of Solow's interest. Gianna and I lifted the heavy wooden boat and gently set it down a few feet away on the weed-infested lot.

Solow gave a woof and I immediately shushed him. He eagerly pawed at the loose dirt. Obviously, someone had been digging in the newly exposed area. Solow went crazy digging holes one after another. We expanded on a couple of Solow's holes until they were about three feet deep. Our shovels simultaneously hit a barrier.

I nervously looked over my shoulder.

No lights and no noise except for the muffled crashing of waves in the distance.

"What is that?" Gianna whispered, as she pointed to the hole in front of her.

I stepped closer and took a look. "Looks like a plastic body bag," I whispered. "It's over here at my end too. Let's dig up the area in between the holes." As I looked into the holes, I realized it was getting easier to see things in the dark. I looked up just as a giant full moon floated up from behind the Waller's rooftop. I was able to see the grimace on Gianna's face and the dirt on Solow's.

Solow didn't need to be asked twice. He was already on the job doing the type of work he was born to do. In his enthusiasm, dirt flew everywhere including at my face.

I coughed and quickly put a hand over my mouth. I looked around to see if anyone heard my cough. I sucked in some air and went back to work. In minutes, we had the whole body bag exposed to moonlight. Our air quality took a real hit, but we persevered anyway. I grabbed one end of the dark plastic bag and Gianna took the other. We half carried, half dragged the thing over to the gate behind the garbage cans.

I hooked Solow's leash to a post and began filling the six-foot-long hole with dirt. Gianna did the same. We carefully lifted the boat and set it back in its original spot. I freed Solow from the post and we dragged the body bag, shovels piled on top, through the gate and down the sidewalk to my truck. The shovels fell to the sidewalk with a clank, clank. We hustled them over to Gianna's back yard and came back for the "bag." Together, we heaved it into the bed of the pickup and I pulled the metal top down tight.

A car drove by.

We froze, looking guiltier than Bratworse clinging to

burning drapes.

"I'll go inside and get our purses," Gianna said.

I heard a car door slam somewhere.

A minute later, Gianna was back, sitting in the passenger seat with Solow scrunched under the dash. I fired up the engine, happy to be leaving the neighborhood. Santa Cruz had gone to bed. We had the roads through town to ourselves for the most part. Just one set of lights in my rearview mirror.

Ten minutes later, I parked the truck at the curb in front of the Police Department. There were no parking problems at one o'clock in the morning—just a couple street people snuggled under a lilac bush next to a rusty shopping cart with mismatched wheels.

I left Solow in the truck while Gianna helped me off-load the body bag. I called it the "bag" because I didn't want to think about what was in it—too much information. We hauled the bag up the brick path, up a couple steps and propped it against the front entrance door. Between the moonlight and the streetlights, Mr. Bag could be seen clearly from the street. I hoped the police would find him in the morning and get right to business.

"Ma'am, is this your vehicle?" a police office walked up to my truck chewing gum.

I was stunned and couldn't speak. Finally, a squeak climbed up out of my throat.

"Yes, officer, it's my truck."

"This is a red zone," he said, pointing to the curb painted red.

"I'm sorry…actually, we were just leaving."

The officer nodded, wished us a good evening and walked down the sidewalk toward Walnut Street.

Gianna climbed into her seat with a giant smile pulling at her lips.

I drove the truck through town, beaming, and then

we were laughing and finally my heart stopped pounding in my ears and I felt light as air. We had accomplished our mission. Now it was up to the police to come up with a name for John Doe and time of death. I was pretty sure I knew both facts already, but it needed to be legal.

***

I wanted to tell David about our close call with the policeman, but I kept it to myself.

"What are you smiling about, Josie?" David asked as his Jeep entered Highway One heading north.

"I was just thinking about how I found a body in the tunnel and a short time later someone stole it. It didn't seem funny at the time, but now I … ah … think it's sort of ironic. Don't you?"

"Hadn't given it much thought, to be honest." He would have to say the *honest* word, as if I didn't already feel guilty.

We bounced along in David's old Jeep from one end of Santa Cruz County to the other with Brat in his cage in the back seat and Solow curled up next to the cage. As we traveled, we talked about things we had packed for the trip and things we forgot. The "forgots" were mostly mine. I had been in such a hurry to feed the boys and myself, shower, pack and think while my mind was stuck back at the police station, it was a wonder I remembered to pack my toothbrush.

I had dropped Gianna at her house at one-fifteen a.m. The neighborhood was still dark except for a gorgeous moon reflecting on the mini-waves and sparkling sand. I made it home a little after two o'clock, wide-awake and giggling to myself about how easy it was to steal a body. Solow looked at me like I'd been drinking fermented apple juice.

"David, if the cabin is too small or icky, let's tell them we can only stay one night."

"Don't worry, Josie. I packed a tent and a camp stove just in case."

We cruised through Ben Lomond and five minutes later, Boulder Creek, a very old logging town that still looked like a very old town with a few logging trucks lumbering through. David made a left at the gas station, the only service station in town, and cruised up the narrow curvy Big Basin Highway. The highway followed the San Lorenzo River as it sliced through two forested mountains. After one mile, we made a sharp right and headed up a curvy mountain road.

"Wow, this is really steep," I said, glancing down the side of the mountain. Cabins appeared wherever there were tiny flat spots to build. The terrain had changed from dark redwood forest to sunny, rocky mountaintop. The road ended at a wide metal gate that slid automatically to the right, out of our way. Ahead was the cabin.

I had imagined a Ma and Pa log cabin in the forest. This was no cabin. The wood-framed house had two stories and a wraparound deck the size of Ben Lomond. We climbed out of the Jeep and stretched. I helped Solow to the ground, and David carried Bratworse's cage.

Before we made it to the front door, Tom and Lois were out the door greeting us enthusiastically. Tom made a fuss over Solow and Lois talked to Brat through the wire.

"Hi, little kitty, kitty," she cooed. She reached for the lock on the cage door.

"I wouldn't do that if I were you, Lois. He's a monster."

"I always wanted a little kitty … but you know how it is with travel and everything," she said, letting go of the lock. "Come in, my dear, and make yourself comfortable."

Our first day with the Trippys consisted of shuffleboard on the deck overlooking whole mountain ranges, meals in local restaurants and a late-night pizza snack delivered to the door. A cruise ship could not have offered more. The difficult part for me was acclimating to a slower pace—no housework, no walls to be painted— just enjoy the moment.

Wednesday morning, I woke with one thing on my mind. I wanted a *Sentinel* newspaper. Would they put a picture of the "bag" propped against the door on the front page? I was dying to know what kind of story they would write about the mysterious reappearance of the body. But most of all, I wondered if the paper would print John Doe's name.

"Tom, I didn't know you could cook," David said as we devoured two stacks of pancakes.

"Actually, this is the only thing I know how to make," Tom laughed, "and Lois makes the batter."

"Tom, do you get a morning paper up here?" I asked.

"No need for a paper. We have an iPad. I'll fix it up for you after breakfast."

David gave me a questioning look.

"I'm just so used to having a newspaper to read in the morning." But in truth, I usually didn't read my paper because I was rushing off to work. Half the time it was David who brought it into the house while I was away. I didn't want to look like I was in a hurry to check the front page, but if I had to wait much longer I was sure I would throw myself off the deck, down the mountain into acres of rocks and brambles.

Half an hour after we finished breakfast, Tom pulled the iPad from a drawer two feet from my elbow. My heart raced as he fussed with it and finally handed it over to me. Because I was electronically challenged, he had to help me get started. I typed in news reports and checked every page of *The Sentinel*. Nothing. Maybe the police wanted to keep the whole thing hush, hush.

One article caught my eye. Jim Waller was being interviewed because Friday night he would announce his candidacy for mayor of Santa Cruz, population 80,000, at the posh Rio Del Mar Convention Center with five hundred of his closest friends. Near the end of the story, Jim was asked about his home life. He talked about golf, Nicki's project to donate eyeglasses to the homeless, and mentioned that his son had recently accepted a good position in Sydney, Australia. I rolled my eyes on that one.

Later in the day, the four of us were discussing plans to drive into Boulder Creek to have lunch at the Café Brewery. I had eaten there before and looked forward to a scrumptious meal. As we were climbing into the Trippy's SUV, my cell phone rang. I didn't feel like answering it, but the thing made so much noise.

"Hello."

"Josephine ..." a quivery voice moaned.

"Gianna? What's the matter?"

"I'm scared. I drove to your house but you weren't there." She sounded like she would fall apart completely, but I couldn't say too much in the Trippy's SUV. "I have terrible news."

"I'm staying with friends in Boulder...." I said.

"Can I come for a visit?" Gianna begged.

"Well, ah ... I don't see why not." I proceeded with directions to the Trippy "cabin" and hung up the phone. A one-hundred-decibel hush permeated the car.

"That was my friend, Gianna. She's menopausal ... and she might show up at the cabin in a couple hours."

An hour and a half later, Gianna's car roared up the mountain and braked in front of the Trippy's hide-away. We had just arrived back at the house from lunch at the Brewery, feeling well fed and relaxed. I walked a few steps from the SUV over to Gianna's car and gave her a hand as she tried to climb out. Her whole body was visibly shaking. Once she was standing, I took her arm and introduced her to David and the Trippys.

"Welcome, dear," Lois said. "I remember those hot flash days. Don't worry—you'll be fine. Come in and relax." She held the front door open for us.

Solow greeted us with a howl, practically tipping Gianna over with surprise.

"I'll just rest here," Gianna said as she flopped down on one of the couches.

I sat beside her, ready to burst if she didn't hurry up and tell me the bad news. How bad could it be?

CHAPTER TWENTY-THREE

My vacation in Boulder Creek included good food, fresh air and David. But Gianna's arrival had stressed me out completely. I was dying to find out what was wrong with Gianna, but Lois had parked her derrière on the sofa next to me. Gianna sat on my right, Lois on my left. How could I politely tell Lois to leave us alone?

I didn't have to worry about the boys because David and Tom were out hiking the near-by trails so that Tom could take pictures of wildlife, if they found any. Other than one hawk, I hadn't seen any wild critters.

"Josephine, I really need to talk to you," Gianna said.

Lois didn't move.

"Maybe we could all share the bad news together," I suggested.

Lois smiled.

"I guess so," Gianna said. She had finally pulled herself together and spoke calmly. "Josephine, I hate to tell you this, but the bag was stolen again."

"You must be kidding," I said.

"You must be kidding," Lois said.

"I'm not kidding, and I'm scared. Monday night, Tuesday morning actually, when you dropped me off at my house, I went upstairs to bed and, minutes later, I heard the Waller's garage door open and close. I was so tired that I didn't think too much of it."

"That's not everything is it?" I said.

"I think the worst is coming," Lois said.

"Last night a noise woke me in the middle of the night. I went to the window—it was like a rerun, but with moonlight this time. Nicki and Jim were digging in the side yard."

I silently strung together the garage door and back yard digging, while Lois rambled on about the benefits of planting a garden in moonlight.

"No wonder there wasn't a story in the newspaper—the bag was re-stolen."

"No wonder." Lois repeated.

"So you can see the danger I'm in. They must have followed us that night. They know that I know … and you know." Gianna shivered.

"You're right. You need a place to stay for awhile," I said.

"You'll stay with us until your menopause attack is over, Lois said.

"Thank you, Lois," … and then came tears of relief.

"Lois, please don't mention any of this to the guys," I said.

"Oh, I never talk about women's problems in mixed company. It's just not done."

I told Gianna she was welcome to stay at my house until things settled down. She thanked me and we agreed that we needed to try again to get the bag back to the police station. In the meantime, we would relax and enjoy our little vacation in Boulder Creek. If sunburn and poison oak were payment for relaxation, I paid my dues.

By Thursday, I was well into vacation-mode, following Solow's example of how to relax. I sat in the shade and read the last three chapters of *Strangled by Silk*, by Barbara Jean Coast while everyone else played shuffleboard on the deck. I had had enough sun and my poison oak required frequent doses of calamine lotion.

By six o'clock, everyone was packed and ready to go home. As a thank you to our host and hostess, David bought dinner at the Brewery. It was a beautiful evening with friends, until I remembered what Gianna and I still needed to do. I visualized the bag under a full moon and shivered.

"What's the matter, Josie?" David asked.

"Just female stuff."

"Oh."

It was eight-thirty when we finally walked to our cars and said good-bye. Gianna followed us forty-five miles to Aromas and up my gravel driveway. David helped me unload my suitcase and bags of cat and dog food while Gianna gently carried my cat and his cage into the house. I showed her the loft, and apologized for the lumpy bed I inherited from my Grandmother.

David and I stepped outside to say goodnight. A long kiss said it pretty well. He wanted to know how long Gianna would be staying with me. I shrugged and told him, "until she's feeling better." He nodded as if he knew all about female problems, and, thanks to Lois, everyone believed Gianna had female problems.

Gianna and I watched the *Ten O'clock News* with Bratworse snoozing on my friend's lap and Solow curled up at my feet. The local news reporter talked about the preparation for Friday night's party at the Rio Del Mar Convention Center and the expected announcement by Jim Waller. We listened to the report and made plans to confiscate the bag while the Wallers were away from home. The only problem was, Gianna lived in a nice area near the beach. People were usually out walking in the evening. We needed a cover, some reason for carrying shovels after dark.

By Friday night, Gianna and I had everything figured out. During the day, we drove to the Feed Store in Aromas and bought a baby lemon tree. When we got home, I loaded my rusty wheelbarrow into the truck along with the lemon tree, a canvas paint tarp and a bottle of bleach. I decided not to take Solow, since we knew exactly where the body was buried. Better not to risk a bark.

The sun went down at eight-thirty, prompting us to get started since the Rio Del Mar function would be ending at ten. We headed to Santa Cruz, a town shrouded in heavy fog. Gianna's neighborhood was sopping with the stuff at nine-thirty. The coastal fog hung low to the ground making visibility about twenty feet. I hoped it would keep the walkers and joggers home where they belonged.

A foghorn groaned somewhere on the bay.

I parked the truck in Gianna's short driveway and unloaded everything to the sidewalk while she went to her back yard for shovels. A minute later, we were creeping up the sidewalk to Nicki's house, the baby lemon tree bouncing along in the wheelbarrow as if Mummy was taking it for a walk in the park. Gianna opened the gate and I pushed the wheelbarrow into the side yard. I dreaded digging up the bag, but it had to be done. Justice had to be done.

I set the little tree to one side. We moved the boat and began digging, fast and hard. We were sweating in the chilly fog, and time was running out. We finally hit the bag with our shovels, worked even harder and dragged John Doe out of the hole. We swung him up into the wheelbarrow, filled the hole and placed the boat carefully in its usual spot. I poured some bleach over the bag and draped the tarp over it, hoping that would cover up the odor of death.

We didn't see any walkers or joggers as Gianna carried the shovels and I pushed the wheelbarrow down the sidewalk to the truck. We loaded the body bag into the truck bed. Gianna quickly parked the wheelbarrow and shovels in her back yard while I yanked the top down over the truck bed.

My little red Mazda rumbled through Santa Cruz

city streets just as the nightlife was heating up. Fog didn't seem to dampen anyone's spirits. The musicians, mimes and ordinary folks were in their favorite spots adding color to the downtown area.

I turned down a side street, pulled into an alley just one building away from the Police Department and cut the engine. As I opened my door, a bicyclist came from behind, weaved and smacked into a wall trying to dodge my door. He and the bike toppled over.

"You can't park here, blankety-blank," he groused.

"So give me a ticket," I snapped.

Gianna put a finger to her lips and shook her head. "Don't make a scene, Josephine."

The guy checked out his bike, hopped on and peddled back where he came from.

We opened the back of the truck and let down the tailgate as quietly as possible. The mixture of chlorine and bad smell stung my eyes. We set the bag down on the pavement and froze as a couple walked by on the sidewalk just fifteen feet away—five feet within the visibility range, and well within the smell zone. They seemed to be very involved in a cozy conversation and ignored us.

"Stay here, Gianna ... act casual. I'll check to see if anyone else is coming." I darted fifteen feet to the sidewalk. The cozy couple had disappeared into the fog and the sidewalk was clear in both directions. I dashed back and helped Gianna carry the bag across the finish line for a second time. It felt like the last hundred feet of a marathon race. Breathing hard, we dropped the bag at the side of the police station instead of at the front entrance since the evening was young and people would be wandering by after dinner or a movie.

As soon as we were back in the truck, we implemented the second part of our two-part plan. I called 911 on my cell phone and reported seeing a body outside the police department over by the Koi pond. Michelle, the 911 operator, asked me to stay on the line. I immediately hug up, fired up the truck and headed across town toward the freeway. Everything was going as planned except....

"By the way, Gianna, you brought the lemon tree back with you, right?"

"No, I thought you had it in the wheelbarrow."

"Darn! Now they're going to know the body is missing," I groaned.

"Not until daylight. Don't worry about it Josephine. By that time, the police will have it." But with our track record, I did worry half the night. Gianna snored away in the loft on a bed not fit for twenty-first century people, while I read a new mystery by Christian Belz. Before I knew it, I had polished off a quart of Rocky Road, half a novel and the sun was beginning to light up the living room.

Gianna pranced down the stairs and stretched her arms. "Thank you, Josephine, for the first sound sleep I've had in a week."

"Don't mention it."

Solow and Brat marched into the room looking fresh and ready for a good run. I let them out and told Gianna to help herself to the shower. As soon as I heard the water running, I hurried down the driveway wearing my robe and slippers, picked up the Friday morning paper and headed back to the house. As I reached the front porch, I noticed a package set against the wall by the door. I picked it up and checked the wrap job, very neatly done like David would do. I set the package on the coffee table, sat down on the sofa and opened the newspaper.

Gianna finished her shower and walked up to me wearing the same clothes she had worn since Wednesday. "Anything interesting in the newspaper today?"

"Nope, not today." I handed it to her. "We should stop over at your house today and pack a bag of clothes for you."

"That would be lovely, Josephine ... that is, if we go together. I wouldn't go alone."

I picked up my package from Mr. Thoughtful and peeled it down to a one-pound box of See's Candy. After a quart of Rocky Road ice cream, I decided to have breakfast before candy. I held the box out to Gianna. "Candy from David," I smiled, wondering when he had had time to shop in Capitola, home of the closest See's Candy store.

"Don't mind if I do," she said, as she snapped up a soft chocolate on chocolate. My favorite piece, actually. I decided to dress and get breakfast started so that I could finally have some candy. My stomach did a happy dance at the thought.

I let Solow and the Brat in and fed them, showered, dressed and came back to the kitchen where Gianna had made coffee and a lovely frittata warmed in the oven. I looked around for my houseguest.

Solow howled and pushed his body against my legs. He howled again and trotted around the corner to the living room where Gianna lay sprawled on the floor. Solow licked her face. She didn't move.

"Oh my God!" I shrieked. "Gianna, what's wrong? Get up, get up." She was breathing but she didn't look good. I ran for the phone and called 911. Help was on the way and I was told to stay on the line. I held that line while I found my cell phone and called David.

David burst through the back door. "Josie, honey, I'm here." He rushed into the living room where I was answering questions from the 911 operator.

"She's a guest in my house ... of course, she didn't eat poison," I said, feeling helpless as I watched

Gianna's color change to pale grey. "Just tell me what I can do to help her," I demanded. My heart pounded as the operator asked more questions and David paced.

CHAPTER TWENTY-FOUR

The longest minutes of my life were finally over when I heard sirens getting louder. Then silence. The EMTs were the first to arrive. I held the door open for them and prayed for a miracle. They went straight to business, hooking Gianna up to an IV and oxygen. I watched from the dining room, leaving them to their work while David paced and took care of practical things like turning off the oven.

I was allowed to sit with Gianna in the ambulance while David drove his Miata over the speed limit to keep up with us. The siren screamed down Highway 129, forcing cars to the edge of the road. It seemed like hours, but only ten minutes passed before we pulled into the back lot at the Watsonville hospital. Earlier, I heard one of the EMTs call in to the hospital asking for a poison expert to be available. Poison? What were they talking about? We hadn't even had breakfast yet.

The back doors opened and I was the first to scurry down the metal ramp. That was the moment I suddenly remembered seeing the open box of candy in the living room. Three pieces were missing. My favorites. Did Gianna have chocolate poisoning? Allergic to chocolate, I wondered. Or did someone put poison in the candy?

David braked his car and leaned his head out the window. "How is she?"

"Nothing's changed. The EMTs think she ate some poison. They were asking me all kinds of questions. By the way, did you give me a box of See's Candy?"

"Not since the box you got for Christmas...."

"Well that's bad news," I said and ran after the EMTs as they rolled Gianna's gurney to the emergency entrance. I caught up to them inside. A woman at the desk pointed me to a waiting area. I sat impatiently as time dragged to a halt. Was Gianna going to live? Was it my fault she was poisoned? Was the poison really meant for me or for both of us? Why wasn't I more careful?

Various scenarios ran through my head. Gianna obviously had enemies. Did she have any other enemies besides the Wallers? Speaking of Wallers, which one was the actual driver/killer? The witness said the driver had blond hair. Did Nicki or her husband wear a blond wig when the rented car crashed through Mario's office walls?

David walked in and sat next to me. He kissed me on my cheek and laid his hand over mine. The combination instantly brought tears to my eyes, which I discretely wiped away with my free hand.

"It's OK to cry, Josie. You've been through a lot," his voice cracked.

My phone startled me out of sad thoughts. It was Fishburn. I told him what had happened to Gianna, and he told me he had news but needed to tell me in person. I told him to meet me at the hospital. We hung up.

Fishburn arrived half an hour later while David was searching the hospital for a sandwich.

"Josephine, have you been crying?" Fishburn sat down in David's chair, reached over and wiped a tear from my cheek.

"We still haven't heard anything on Gianna's condition," I said.

Fishburn stood up and walked the ten feet to the desk, showed his badge and asked about Mrs. Portello. I couldn't hear what the nurse said, but the smile on her face seemed like a good sign. Fishburn sat down in

David's seat and reported that Gianna was stable and the doctors thought she would recover.

I breathed a huge sigh, and let go of the hundred-pound weights on my shoulders.

"Josephine, you wouldn't by chance know who poisoned your friend?"

"Her neighbor doesn't like her. At some point, you might see a connection between her neighbor, Nicki Waller, and the murderer."

Fishburn raised his eyebrows and leaned closer to my ear. "Ms. Stuart, you wouldn't happen to know who recovered the body?"

"You found the body? That's great. Who is it?" I asked, as if I didn't know.

"It was twenty-seven-year-old James P. Waller the second. We found his wallet in his pocket and a gun was still in his hand. It might have been Mr. Portello's way of showing that the boy had pulled a gun on him, they struggled and the gun went off."

"Any idea who Mario's murderer is?" I asked. "Obviously, it's not young Waller."

"We're checking the gun registration. That might shine a light on someone. Now, Josephine, tell me exactly what happened with this poison thing," Fishburn said.

"This morning I was bringing my newspaper in the house, but just as I got to the front door something caught my eye. It was a shiny silver package the size of a one-pound candy box. It was See's Candy, actually, and everyone knows it's my favorite. I didn't give it a second thought. I just assumed David left it for me."

"You mean that guy?" Fishburn nodded toward David who was walking toward us.

"Sergeant, don't get the wrong idea. David wouldn't hurt anyone."

I looked up at David coming closer, eating a

sandwich. He sat down on the other side of me and the guys shook hands across my mid-section. The smell of ham sandwich had me squirming. My breakfast never happened and lunchtime had arrived. But David had not forgotten me. When all the sharing of information was over and Fishburn walked away, David pulled a wrapped sandwich from his shirt pocket and handed it to me.

"It sounds to me like you two know who poisoned Mrs. Portello," David said, looking straight into my red-rimmed eyes.

"We have a hunch, but no proof. It seems Gianna didn't get along with her neighbor. I guess we can leave now. The doctor said she has a good chance."

"OK, but one question, if her neighbor doesn't like her, why drop the package at your house?"

David had a point. I silently took the fifth and another bite from my sandwich. He had pinpointed the really scary fact that someone knew Gianna was staying at my house. Maybe they hoped to kill both of us with a poisoned chocolate binge.

We left the hospital and rode home in the Miata with the top down. I invited David in for a glass of lemonade. It would be our first time alone in a very long time, since we had had no real privacy at the cabin. He stayed for dinner but left in an awkward silence after Bratworse toppled an antique train lantern onto his head. I wondered if the Brat had climbed to the highest shelf and calculated the right moment when David walked by.

Feeling the after-glow of my magical afternoon with David, except for the last five minutes, I left the house and drove straight to Watsonville Hospital. I found Gianna propped up in her bed with an IV in her arm and a monitor tab stuck to her chest.

"Gianna, are you awake?"

Her eyes opened. "Josephine, thank you for coming." Her color wasn't normal, but it wasn't too bad considering what had happened. "Anything new?"

"I talked to Fishburn today. I'm pretty sure he knows we're the ones who recovered the bag. They identified John Doe with a driver's license for James P. Waller II, and they're checking out the gun. Does Jim Waller own a gun?"

"I don't know. They were my neighbors for fourteen years, but one never knows what goes on behind closed doors," she sighed.

"Gianna, I was wondering something … has Nicki ever been a blond?"

"As a matter of fact, she was for many years, but recently she had her hair dyed brown, her real color. She said blond was too much trouble to take care of. Did you find out anything about who poisoned me?"

A nurse walked in and checked Gianna's chart.

"We think the poison was in the candy. Sergeant Fishburn wants to get fingerprints off the box. He said he would be over to pick up the box this evening. I said I could bring it to the station, but he insisted on coming out to Aromas at nine o'clock this evening."

The nurse lingered—all ears.

Gianna raised an eyebrow, "Sounds like he has a crush on you."

"Oh no, I already told him about David. Do you really think he has a crush on me?" I blushed.

The nurse smiled and walked out. I was the next to leave after wishing Gianna a quick recovery. I still had an hour before the Fishburn appointment so I stopped at the market for some fresh salad material. As I walked the ice cream aisle, Robert called to me from the pizza section of the freezer he was stocking.

"Hey, Robert, what's new?"

"I heard a report on KPIG that the stolen body

showed up at the police department." He cocked his head as if I might be able to add to that piece of news.

"Really, how interesting." I dropped a tub of peach swirl and a frozen apple pie into my cart. "Don't look at me like that—I couldn't tell you if I wanted too. You talk too much." Immediately I regretted my words.

Robert was silent as he went back to his stocking job.

I walked over to him. "Robert, I didn't mean that like it sounded. I just meant that so far only two people actually know what happened to the body." I whispered.

Robert whipped his body around to face me. "You are the one, aren't you? Somehow I knew it would be you...."

"Shh! OK, now you know, just keep it to yourself. This whole thing is going to explode real soon." Robert looked so serious I almost told him it was all a joke. But he knew me. He knew it was no joke. But the lady shopping at the other end of the aisle didn't know me, and she gave me a look like I had just busted out of the sanitarium.

As I drove home, I thought about what I would say to the Sergeant. One thought was to tell him everything I knew. The second was to shrewdly take my time with a wait-for-more-information attitude. I would serve him a plate of pie and ice cream, and he would be putty in my artistic hands.

As I drove up the driveway, my sweet little adobe house had taken on the colors of a gorgeous sunset. Looking east, the purple going black parts of sky already had twinkly stars. What a magnificent evening—a nice ending to a day that had started off so horribly.

Even as I was admiring the sky and petting Solow and Brat, a car swished to a stop behind my truck. The red lights weren't flashing, but Fishburn and his partner looked way too serious.

CHAPTER TWENTY-FIVE

Early Sunday morning I gave up trying to sleep and headed for the kitchen and good old Mr. Coffee. Strong cups of caffeine would help cheer me and Officer Dirkson who slept contentedly on my sofa with a quarter of his body hanging over one end. The nine o'clock evening meeting with Fishburn had given me my very own bodyguard—a twenty-two-year-old rookie named Shortie. I was told that I had to keep him until the Wallers could be located.

Saturday night, Sergeant Fishburn told me that the Wallers had been spotted in Santa Cruz by an elderly woman.

I pumped him for the name of the lady.

Finally he caved, checked his little notebook and told me her name was Myrtle Roundwell.

"Oh no, not Myrtle!" My heart bumped up to full-speed. "Were the Wallers right there in her neighborhood?"

"Walnut Street. I can't tell you any more than that."

"Oh, yes you can because my parents live next door to Myrtle. I need to know if they're all right," I choked.

"Calm down, Josephine. Myrtle said your folks are out of town for a bowling competition."

"Sergeant, did you know that Jim Waller is on my Dad's bowling team?"

"I'll make a note of it. In the meantime, Shortie will keep you safe and we have an APB out on the Wallers. I'll take the box of candy with me, and we'll check for prints. Don't worry, Josephine, everything is going to be all right." Fishburn took the box I handed him, leaving his hand on mine a little longer than necessary. He dropped the box into an evidence bag.

My cheeks reddened. I told him to be careful and wished him luck.

Fishburn opened the door to leave.

A lanky young man stood on the porch with a cigarette in his mouth.

"Josephine, this is Officer Dirkson. Shortie, stow that butt—it'll stunt your growth."

"Yes, sir; nice to meet you, ma'am." He squished the butt with his highly polished shoe and walked inside as the sergeant walked in the other direction, down the driveway to his cruiser.

"So, Shortie, what do you know about this case?" I asked, looking up to the ceiling.

"I'm kinda new around here, just got transferred from Fresno."

"Well, make yourself at home. There's a bed upstairs in the loft and the couch down here.

"Don't worry about me, ma'am. I'll be keeping watch all night."

I toddled off to bed by myself since Solow and Bratworse wanted to stay with the stranger who kept fussing over them. I took the phone with me and called Mom and Dad. No one picked up so I left a short message. I called their cell phones. No answer. Maybe they went to bed early, but that wouldn't be normal. I tried calling again Sunday morning. Still no answer!

I tried to console myself with the fact that Jim was running for Mayor, so, of course, people would know what he looked like. He would be easy to find. But when morning's first light appeared, I had slept very little, and my worries had increased. What if Mom and Dad were tangled up in this terrible mess? I picked up the phone and dialed Myrtle's number. The phone rang many times.

"Hello."

"Myrtle, it's me, Josephine. I heard that you saw the Wallers yesterday. What's going on?"

"Is this Tony? Hang on, Tony, while I get my hearing aids." She came back to the phone. "OK, Tony, this better be important...."

"Myrtle, it's Josephine and it is important. Did you see Mom and Dad yesterday?"

"Maybe, dear, but I'm not sure. I had just finished watching KPUT *News at Noon*. I went to the kitchen for a glass of water and glanced out the window. I had just seen the Wallers on TV, and there they were getting out of a cab. They went straight to your mom's front door."

"Is that all you saw?" I asked.

"About five minutes later, I came back to the kitchen to make my lunch. I saw Jim getting into the driver's seat of your dad's green Oldsmobile. I thought that was peculiar and called the police."

"It's actually a blue Buick, but never mind. Did you see anything else? Were Jim and Nicki the only ones in the car?"

"I didn't get a good look at how many people were in the car; it pulled away so fast, heading west, or did I already say that? Oh tiddlywinks, I just stepped on Whiskers' paw. Now he's mad at me."

"Back to my next question, did you tell the Sergeant that you saw the Wallers in Dad's car?" I wanted to shout into her hearing aid, but instead I tried to sound calm so that Myrtle would be able to think clearly, possibly for the first time in her long life.

"Well, dear, I remember saying something about the Wallers walking up the sidewalk and knocking on your parent's door ... but Whiskers jumped up on the table and I yelled at him. I'm sorry, Josephine, I don't remember if I told the police about your dad's car," she apologized.

"Thanks, Myrtle; I'll see you in an hour or so." I hung up and quickly dressed myself. I offered to buy Shortie a fast food breakfast if he would follow me out to the truck. Like a starving puppy, Shortie couldn't resist. He set his little butt on the passenger seat, then hauled one leg at a time into the cab and crammed them in front of the dash with knees up to his chin.

I turned the key and looked over at my new friend. "Sorry, Shortie, for the limited space."

"No worries. My mom's a yoga instructor. I can do this," he smiled.

The drive to Santa Cruz was slow, lots of beach goers on the road, not to mention people on their way to various entertainments like the strawberry festival, mushroom festival, barbeque cook-off, wharf-to-wharf race, save the snails cook-off, pizza throwing contest and the tuba concert at the River Park.

I finally made it to Mom's neighborhood. As I turned down Walnut Street, I saw Mom's Subaru parked in front of their house, but no big blue Buick. I pulled in behind the Subaru, in front of Myrtle's gas-guzzler, and decided to check on Myrtle first. She let us in and offered us a piece of berry cobbler from the oven. I decided that Mom's house could wait a little longer after watching Myrtle load each piece of cobbler with a serious amount of whipped cream.

"Josephine, who's this handsome young fellow you have here?"

"Sorry; this is my bodyguard, Officer Dirkson. Shortie, this is my friend Myrtle." I ate one piece of berry cobbler in the time it took Shortie to eat two pieces. As soon as we finished, we excused ourselves and walked next door. I lifted a pot of geraniums sitting by the front door and used the hidden key to gain entrance. I felt eyes on my back and looked behind us.

"Come on, Myrtle; we'll all go in together."

"So that's where they keep the key," Myrtle said. "Your mother told me the hiding place in case they weren't home and I needed a cup of sugar or something, but I forgot what she told me. So many things to remember, twiddle dee ... oh, no, Josephine. It looks like something happened in the living room. Look, the lamp toppled over ... oh dear."

Shortie instantly had his gun in hand as he cautiously crept from room to room. When he finally came back to the living room with an "all clear" message, I took my first deep breath in what seemed like an eternity. I had worried the whole time that he might find my parents wounded or worse.

Where would the Wallers go? The police would be looking for them from border to border. The border? I grabbed Mom's phone and dialed the Watsonville Hospital.

"Hello, my name is Josephine Stuart and I need to talk to Gianna Portello right away about a life and death problem ... please."

At first, the receptionist resisted my request by talking about rules in the ER and such.

"Let me talk to your supervisor," I demanded.

"I'll connect you to the patient's room, but your request is highly irregular and your manner is impudent."

"Hello? This is Mrs. Portello...."

"Gianna, this is Josephine. We think my parents might have been kidnapped by the Wallers. Tell me as quickly as you can the name of Nicki's cleaning lady. Didn't you say she spends half the year in Mexico?"

"Yes, that's right. Her name is Elena something. I'm sorry but I don't think I ever did know her last name."

"Do the Wallers happen to have an extra key outside their house somewhere?"

"I know there's one on the back patio under a large metal frog near the back door to the garage. Be careful, Josephine." We hung up.

Shortie and I ran to the truck with just a quick wave to Myrtle.

"Go get 'em, Josephine!" she wailed from the front door.

Shortie pulled out his police phone and then stuffed himself into my little pickup. He quickly contacted Fishburn. We arrived at the Waller house simultaneously. Mr. Blue Eyes listened to my idea. He even used the froggy key to enter the house. He said it was a long shot, but it was all we had.

"I'll look upstairs," Fishburn said. "Shortie, check the downstairs for a Rolodex or an address book. Hope the Wallers are old-fashioned enough to still have things like that," the sergeant said as he took the stairs two at a time.

Shortie riffled through the desk in the den while I rummaged through the little built-in desk in the kitchen.

I found a well-used address book in the top drawer. "Hey, you guys, I found something," I shouted. Shoes pounded down the stairs and Shortie hurried to my side. I thumbed through the book searching for Elena. When I got to the R's, I found Elena Rico. We all high-fived each other over finding the Santa Cruz address and phone number.

"Probably not a good idea to call...." Fishburn mumbled.

"Look," I said. "She lives on Twenty-first Avenue, that's only two minutes from here, up the hill and around the corner." The three of us scrambled into the cruiser with me in the back seat. A couple of minutes later, we were parked in a patch of dead grass in front of a small summer house, converted into year-round-living like most of the other old houses on the block.

The biggest and best two houses were the ones at the end of the street over-looking the ocean.

Fishburn told Shortie to get out of the car and walk the driveway to the back door. When Long Legs disappeared around the corner behind a very old unattached single-car garage, Fishburn told me to stay in the car, climbed out of the cruiser and walked to the front door. I watched the Sergeant unclip his holster.

CHAPTER TWENTY-SIX

The front door opened, Fishburn entered the little house and the weathered door closed behind him. My anxiety level was off the charts. What was happening in that house? Minutes passed. My fingernails were chewed down to the nub. I stared at the front porch so hard I thought it might catch fire. If the sergeant went inside to get an address from Elena, he could have done it twenty times over. Something didn't feel right.

I climbed out of the cruiser and closed the door quietly, hoping the sound of the ocean would dull the metal-on-metal clank. Hunched over, I ran down the dirt driveway, noticing that the house window blinds were all in the down position. I went to the backside of a very old one-car garage and found a place where two boards had separated from each other leaving a half-inch crack for me to peek into.

I sensed someone was watching me from the road. I should have been watching him. He was young, blond, tanned and half naked. He struggled with his wetsuit and finally pulled it off completely. I tried to turn my head away, but it was frozen in shock or something. He quickly wrapped a beach towel around his waist and climbed into his red VW bus with surfboards strapped to the top and drove away.

"No harm done," I told myself and put my eyeball up to the crack in the garage wall. It was dark inside. I gave my eye a moment to adjust. Eventually, I was able to make out a shiny object, one that stopped my heart, then sent it ticking off balance like the clock in Alice in Wonderland. I was staring at the chrome figure my dad had mounted on the hood of his car. It was a man crouching as he leans forward just about to let go of a bowling ball, a figure taken from his very first bowling trophy.

I figured chances were a hundred to none my parents were inside the house with Fishburn and some really awful people. I took a couple deep breaths, crept ten feet over to the back of the house and looked around for Shortie.

He found me first and I jumped a foot.

"Shortie, you need to call for back-up right away," I whispered.

"I was just about to do that. Here, hold my gun."

He pushed the revolver into my right hand, which suddenly began shaking uncontrollably. Shortie called in for help, while I pointed the gun at the back door. I heard voices getting louder and something like a wooden chair being slammed against a wall. Obviously, Fishburn didn't have the upper hand, or he would have come outside with the Wallers at gunpoint. I heard footsteps and watched the doorknob turn.

"They're coming," I whispered as I ducked behind a garbage can.

Shortie didn't move fast enough, and he didn't have access to a gun. The door flew open, and he was immediately marched into the house at the end of Jim's shotgun. Wasn't Jim Waller the guy at city hall preaching about gun control? The door slammed and all was quiet.

What should I do? My own mother and father were in there. I couldn't go in and possibly get them killed. I couldn't stay outside and do nothing.

Once I was able to get my shaky legs moving, I rounded the house and began walking east, up Twenty-first Avenue toward East Cliff, hoping to intercept our back-up police. The neighborhood was quiet except for the pounding of waves and my heartbeat. Maybe I would find the surfer dude and ask him for help. I could hold the gun; he would be a decoy.

A police car turned off East Cliff Drive and headed west on Twenty-first Avenue straight to where I was wildly waving my whole arm, just two houses away from Elena's place. They screeched to a stop. A door flew open.

"Ma'am, drop the gun."

"Huh? Oh, sure." I dropped it like my hand was on fire. "It's that little blue house...."

"Ma'am, put your hands up."

"Yes, sir, but you better hurry...." I respectfully raised my hands into the air. "My elderly parents are hostages."

One of the two officers picked up the gun, sniffed it and felt it for heat. He cuffed my hands behind my back and stuffed me into the back seat of the patrol car before I had time to explain my mission. The car rolled fifty feet closer to Elena's and stopped. One officer cracked my window open.

"They have Officers Dirkson and Fishburn in the...." I said as the doors slammed and I was alone. Minutes ticked by. I couldn't chew my nails because they were behind my back. Somewhere between five and fifteen minutes went by. It's hard to tell time in a stressful situation.

I watched one officer sneak up to the front door while his partner went to the back of the house. Nothing new in that strategy, I thought, remembering the old cowboy and detective movies.

Feeling desperate, my shoulders caved and my head dropped as I prayed for help. What else could I do?

"Hallo."

I turned my head. "Who are you?" I said to a little girl about seven years old.

"Are you a quiminal?"

"No I'm not. They just don't want me interfering with stuff," I explained.

"You look like a quiminal."

I decided to ignore her and looked away, noticing that the front porch was empty. It seemed to me the police needed a distraction, some outside help.

"What's your name, little girl?"

"Angel. I live with Gwanma Elena over there." She pointed to the little blue house.

"Angel, how would you like to help your Grandma?"

Angel nodded her pig-tailed head. "I will help Gwanma," she said, giving me a glimpse of the space where two new teeth were coming in.

"OK, you have to do this real fast. Can you run fast?"

"I won vewy fast."

"You look around and pick up the biggest two rocks you can find. Got that?"

"Two big wocks," she repeated.

"You carry the wocks, I mean rocks to your Grandma's front porch and throw them through the window, and then run back to me really fast, OK."

Angel laughed and shook her head. "No, no!"

"Yes, yes. Your Grandma is in danger. Am I sitting in a police car? Is that another police car over there?"

Angel nodded her head, looking very serious. "OK, bye, lady." She shuffled along the sidewalk looking into someone's unattended patch of dirt, picking up rock after rock, examining each one and tossing it away.

"Angel," I shouted, "find two rocks quickly."

She stooped over and picked up two rocks, sprinted twenty yards to Elena's porch and threw the rocks like a jock. One rock made it through a window. Angel whirled around and headed back to the patrol car.

I heard a shot.

People poured out of the house like bees from a hive. The last two out the door were the two officers who had captured me. But my mother and father were not in the group. My heart was breaking.

"Lady, I boke a window...." Angel looked worried.

"I know, honey. You did a good job—not that you'll ever need to do this again in your life."

I watched the Wallers being cuffed and stowed in the back seat of Fishburn's cruiser. Shortie saw me and encouraged one of the officers to stroll over to the car and uncuff me. As the cuffs came off and I was released, I called to Fishburn.

The sergeant met me halfway. "We didn't find your parents, but we'll keep looking," he said as he put a hand on my shoulder, probably expecting me to break into tears.

"Has anyone looked in the garage?" I asked.

"Not yet, but of course we will look there." We walked together to the garage. Fishburn pulled the door open while I scurried inside for a look. Mom and Dad were in a pile on the back seat, their hands and feet tied. Were they asleep, or...?"

"Move back, Josephine. I'll check this out," Fishburn said, but I already had my hand on Mom's throat, and I wasn't about to move. Her skin was warm and I felt her blood pumping through her veins. I moved my hand to Dad's ankle. Same thing—warm skin, blood pumping.

Fishburn called for EMTs and an ambulance.

Angel pulled her Grandma Elena over to meet me.

"Josephine, ees nice to meet you. Does Wallers ees bad peoples. Now I will look for a better place to work," she smiled. We chatted for a few minutes as I kept my eyes on the back seat of the Buick until the EMTs arrived. They assured me that my parents had been drugged and would sleep it off. But, of course, they would be examined and taken care of at the hospital. Mom and Dad were loaded into the Medivac vehicle and sirens wailed up the street and turned onto East Cliff Drive.

Fishburn said he would drive me back to my truck. I rode shotgun while the Wallers fumed in the back seat, handcuffed and irate. Mr. Blue Eyes walked me to my truck and handed me one of his cards.

"If you ever find yourself alone...."

I handed the card back to him. "I know where to find you. Thanks for capturing Mario's killer." I turned and climbed into the driver's seat of my sweet little truck. The whole world seemed brighter, happier. The EMTs said Mom and Dad would be OK. All I had to do was drive to Dominican Hospital and make sure they had everything they needed.

After that, I would drive home and invite David over because he was all I needed.

EPILOGUE

It was time for me to decompress, lighten up and be David's girl again. Things had worked out pretty well, except for the Wallers. Nicki was going to trial for murder, and her husband was accused of harboring a fugitive (his wife) plus a few incidentals like stealing a body, poisoning Gianna and kidnapping my parents. A portion of my taxes would be helping to pay for their rooms and three squares a day.

Gianna was getting her life together. She joined a quilting club, a gardening club and adopted Bratworse. She said she loved the kitten from the first time she saw him, which would have been right after he ripped the shoulder off her silk blouse. I didn't understand it; but I let Bratworse go, knowing he would be happier with Gianna. We discussed the poisoning of the dogs and she finally agreed to keep it to herself. What was done was done. Santa Cruz jurors were more likely to let a murderer off with a light sentence, but there would be no mercy for killing two little dogs.

Gianna donated three of Mario's paintings to the Santa Cruz Art League Gallery on Broadway. The write-up in *The Sentinel* was fabulous. Maybe people would see his talent and sensitivity in the paintings and remember him in a better light.

Alicia, Ernie, Trigger, David and I attended a roller derby meet at the new Kaiser Stadium. We enjoyed comfortable seats, air conditioning and met up with old friend spectators, Bonnie and Ashley. Santa Cruz squashed Silicon Valley, thrilling us with their cunning and dexterity.

Mom and Dad took Myrtle's RV to the Grand Canyon while Myrtle stayed home and taught me the intricacies of poker. It was fun, but I lost my favorite bracelet in the process—the price of knowledge.

Speaking of fun, David took me on a trip to Hawaii. He looked wonderful on the beach, in the pool, on the boat, at the hotel. We had nothing to argue about—at first. Not until the owner of the boat we rented was found dead in the hallway outside our door. Suddenly everyone in the hotel looked like a suspect to me. David wanted the trip to end right away, and I wanted to extend our vacation so I would have time to solve the murder, naturally. I guess it's that old "opposites attract" thing.

THE END

ABOUT THE AUTHOR

 As a retired muralist and commercial artist, Joyce Oroz has an abundance of painting experiences she infuses into Josephine's adeventures. Oroz say, "Writing is like painting a series of pictures without the messy paint." She spends her time writing mysteries, a blog and monthly newspaper articles. She is happily settled in Aromas, California, with her husband, also a writer, and their Labrador retriever. ROLLER RUBOUT is her second mystery with Cozy Cat Press.

Also by Joyce Oroz:

Secure the Ranch
Read My Lipstick
Shaking In Her Flip Flops
Beetles in the Boxcar
Cuckoo Clock Caper

www.ingramcontent.com/pod-product-compliance
Lightning Source LLC
Chambersburg PA
CBHW020319260626
47156CB00004B/1294